CHRISTMAS COMES TO ODDLETON

DULCIE FEENAN

Christmas Comes to Oddleton
Copyright © 2012 Dulcie Feenan

Kindle Edition
ISBN: 978-1-908212-11-5

ISBN: 978-1-908212-11-5

✤ Created with Vellum

THE TWELVE DAYS OF CHRISTMAS

For Mrs. Troyd, the whole point of Christmas was the Nativity play. A woman referred to as "formidable" by the charitable (and "a battleaxe" by the rest), for many years this paragon of iron will had been something of a legend among the other school staff. The Nativity play was the highpoint of Mrs. Troyd's year, and as such was her own especial project. As soon as school started in September, she watched the children to see who would make a good Joseph, which one could hold a tune well enough to be Mary, and who could not be trusted to learn or retain their lines—or indeed to say them at the right time. As soon as the excitement of Halloween was over and the black and orange tissue paper taken down from the classroom walls, Mrs. Troyd would choose from her plays, and letters would go out to the parents.

Letters were not enough in some cases, but Mrs. Troyd was accomplished in her dealings with the more recalcitrant parent. She attended the church every Sunday, always sitting in the second pew on the right-hand side, and the minute the last notes of the final hymn began to fade, Mrs. Troyd whisked down the aisle ready to lie in wait for her unsuspecting victim in the front hall of the church.

This particular morning she was there ready and waiting for the Grant family.

"Ah, there you are Stephanie," she trilled as the small child stepped through the door. "And you must be Stephanie's mother?"

"Yes, I am."

Mrs. Troyd stepped forward to shake her hand, neatly blocking them in the doorway. "Ah, splendid. I wanted to talk to you about the Christmas play. The letters went out but yours must have gone awry, I suspect, as I haven't had Stephanie's form back yet."

"Ah, yes, the Christmas play..." Mrs. Grant shifted slightly to let someone past, but the doorway was too small. There was something of a queue building up behind her, but Mrs. Troyd was in the way and she could not come forward or back.

"Now, I have decided that Stephanie would make a splendid Sheep in the Nativity. I know she's very excited about it, aren't you Stephanie?" Mrs. Troyd did not wait for an answer. "All the children have been playing Nativities in the playground, bless them, and they're really looking forward to being involved. Now, the rehearsals are after Mass on Sundays, for an hour, and the Nativity itself will be at 7 o'clock on Christmas Eve, just before the Vigil Mass."

"I'm not sure that Stephanie wants to be in the play though," Stephanie's mother objected feebly. "She hasn't mentioned it to me."

"Oh but of course she does—don't you Stephanie?" Mrs. Troyd fixed the child with a basilisk glare.

"Would you like to be a sheep in the play, dear?" Mrs. Grant asked.

Stephanie cast a slightly hunted look from one to the other, then with two adults staring at her, one of whom was more than a little bit alarming, she took the easiest way out. "Er... Yes?"

Mrs. Troyd beamed. "Splendid. I'll see you next Sunday at the first rehearsal, shall I?" She stepped aside to let Mrs. Grant and Stephanie go on their way, then rummaged in her capacious handbag and extracted a small flowery diary in which she put a big tick next to Stephanie's name. Then, satisfied, she made her way back into the church to pick up her bag and coat.

On the way she met Maria Effle.

"Morning Mrs. T," that lady began. "I bin meaning to have a word with you about the Christmas play."

"Ah yes, we must get together and talk about the costumes," Mrs. Troyd acknowledged, not stopping. "I have to be off now, but I'll arrange something in the next week or two."

"Well, you see, I have a problem with the last week of rehearsals…"

"Oh don't worry, Maria, you don't have to be at the rehearsals that last week, so long as we can get the costumes together in time for the dress rehearsal. If we need to we can have a costume check the previous week." Mrs. Troyd scooped up her coat and bag and turned back to the door.

"Well it's just it would worry me, the idea that I might be lettin' you all down. I thought you might like to find someone else to do it this year," Maria called after her. "It might be easier, that's all."

"Of course you wouldn't be letting us down, Maria. And don't worry, we won't be replacing you. What would we do without our Costumes Mistress?" Beaming over her shoulder, Mrs. Troyd hurried out the door.

"Costumes Mistress?" Maria glared at the statue of St. Francis next to her. "I only offered to sew up Joseph's hem cos I thought he would trip over it, an' that were four years back! Well, I did try at least, this year."

But St. Francis was not to be drawn and preserved a discreet silence.

* * *

A FELLOW-SUFFERER in this respect was Nell Pettit, an older parishioner who had offered to prompt for the play some six years back and never managed to extricate herself since. Her portfolio of duties was varied and growing with every year. There was always the trouble of making sure that the children attended the pertinent rehearsals, of course, and this being an ongoing battle, Mrs. Troyd had graciously delegated this to Nell some two years back. This year was rendered particularly problematic by the fact that the le Grand family had taken it into their heads to go on an unexpected skiing holiday prior to the play.

At the end of the practice before they went, Arianna came up to Nell with the twins. "We're off now, Nell; we'll see you in three weeks."

"Three weeks?" Nell's voice squeaked with dismay, so she cleared her throat again. "Whatever do you mean?"

"Oh, did I not tell you, dear?" Arianna smiled graciously. "How remiss of me. We're going on a skiing holiday for the next three weeks. We bought it last minute so we got an awfully good deal on a luxury chalet in the Italian Alps. They say George Clooney was there last year, you know. Of course celebs don't go to the same place twice, but as I told the children, if it's good enough for George, it's good enough for us!"

"Three weeks?"

"Well, yes, dear, but we'll be back in time for the dress rehearsal. I don't think it should be a problem though; Suzanna and Alex will be perfectly able to play their roles as the Angel Gabriel and the Third King. There will be plenty of time to learn their lines on holiday and they will have the dress rehearsal to refresh their memories—although the little darlings, being from theatrical stock, are so quick that they will most likely remember it after the first run-through. Now, I'm afraid we have to dash. Skis to pack, you know!"

Arianna leant forward to do air-kisses at the startled Nell, who watched with a sinking heart as mother and children wafted up the aisle and away. She was fairly sure that Arianna had not passed on this small but vital snippet of information to Mrs. Troyd, and this being the case, Nell knew exactly who the messenger was who was about to get shot.

"Mrs. Troyd, did Arianna have a word with you?"

"No..." Mrs. Troyd looked up, hackling in expectation. Nell passed this information on to Mrs. Troyd with a certain amount of gloomy trepidation, and as expected, that lady had not taken it at all well.

"Those benighted le Grands!" Mrs. Troyd wailed, shaking a dimpled fist at the heavens. "Every year! That woman does it on purpose, and it's perfectly clear why!"

"Er... is it?" Nell was startled into making an unwary reply and received a poisonous look for her pains.

"Of course it is, Nell! I know that your generation was much more upright and naïve than mine and it's very endearing but surely, surely even an innocent like you can see that Arianna le Grand has designs upon my Nativity play!"

"Designs? What sort of designs?" Knowing Arianna only slightly, Nell was inclined to think that these would involve some kind of heavy silk brocade, possibly in a slightly scandalous shade of scarlet, whereas Mrs. Troyd, if she were associated with any designs at all, would probably be something floral with frills and matching scatter cushions. In fact, if she had been a sofa, Nell suspected Mrs. Troyd would have been one of those upright horsehair efforts that looked quite comfortable but generally proved slightly less yielding than the average piece of granite.

"Designs, Nell!" Mrs. Troyd's tones vibrated with all the loathing available to a dramatic alto. "I should have thought that it is common knowledge that when I first suggested the idea of putting on a yearly Nativity play, that woman maintained that she had first come up with the idea and should be in charge of proceedings, citing her own experience as an opera singer! Poor woman, she clearly assumes that singing on her own a couple of times in a parochial little company qualifies her as some kind of teacher, whereas clearly what is needed is someone who has years of experience with children and can inspire them. They are too young to learn to sing like Pavarotti, but with the right tuition, they may be inspired to be the next Shirley Temple!"

Shirley Temple? God forbid, thought Nell, and realised she was speaking. "Oh, it wasn't a little local company, Mrs. Troyd, it was the Calliope Touring Opera. They opened Glyndebourne when she was playing Tosca, you know, which is a very great honour!"

"Tosca!" From the darkening of Mrs. Troyd's brow, it was clear that this was the wrong answer. "I've never heard of it! I daresay it's one of these filthy modern travesties that shock their way into theatres for ten minutes and then are never heard of again! Besides, no respectable company would name itself after a steam organ—so uncouth!"

Nell sighed. A steam organ! These days if there was one child in twenty that knew their Homer, you were surprised, but in her day, every child had been taught the classics, and she had assumed that Mrs. Troyd would also have known this. "Well, Arianna has promised faithfully that Suzanna and Alex will learn their lines, and they are very good; but if you want to give their parts to some of the other children, I'm sure no one would wonder at it."

"No! I shan't give her that pleasure! And in all honesty, I don't think any of the other children could do the Angel Gabriel as well as Suzanna." Mrs. Troyd's face softened. "I have to say, for a girl with a mother like that, Suzanna is a wonderful child, and so pretty with those blond curls! And she sings so beautifully! She'll be a real asset to this play, Nell, so we mustn't think of replacing her. As for Alex, he's only playing the Third King—poor boy, with a twin as brilliant as Suzanna, he will always find it difficult to compete. And good-looking as he is, he just hasn't got anything like her talent. No, Nell, we will leave the le Grands with their roles and simply trust that they have enough pride in themselves to do the part justice."

The le Grand twins being mischievous at best, and all of eight years of age, Nell couldn't help thinking that this was possibly an unwise course of action. But once Mrs Troyd had made a decision, she would continue on her course with the massive inevitability of a tectonic plate. Contradiction was pointless, but Nell had long since developed ways of steering her instead. "Very well, but perhaps we might let some of the other children learn the lines? Just for convenience in the practices, you understand, and only the ones who would be offstage at the time anyway."

Mrs. Troyd considered this briefly. "My thought entirely; I was about to suggest just that. We will do so at the very next practice."

And true to her word, at the next practice Mrs. Troyd sent Nell to sort out the understudies while she herself discussed the important question of costumes with Maria Effle.

THE ANGEL GABRIEL FROM HEAVEN CAME

"Children! Children!" Nell flapped her hands at the crowd of children who gathered around. Nell did not have Mrs. Troyd's presence or teacher's voice, but the children liked her and generally did as she asked, albeit in their own sweet time. Now they chattered and laughed between themselves for a moment longer before falling quiet to see what she had to say.

"Children, as you know Alex and Suzanna will be on holiday for a few weeks, and when they aren't there to take part in the rehearsals, we will need someone to speak the lines for the Angel Gabriel. Would anyone like to be an understudy for Suzanna?"

"Me, Miss! Please, Miss I want to do it! Let me, Miss, I'd learn all the words all right!"

Nell frowned. This was a little tricky. "Michael, the Angel is a part that is more usually played by a girl. Really I was hoping one of the girls would do the part. We only have a few boys, so we need you to be the Innkeeper."

Michael jutted his chin out obstinately. "I don't want to be the innkeeper, Miss, the innkeeper is boring. The innkeeper only gets to say 'no'. I want to be the angel, with the tinsel, and tell Mary she's up the duff and all that."

"Up the...?"

"Means pregnant, Miss."

"I know it means pregnant, Michael, but it is a very coarse way of saying it and we are in church, so let us agree that Mary is pregnant and not up the duff, shall we? Also, I'm sorry but the Angel Gabriel is a girl so I don't see how you can be the Angel Gabriel. Patty, you could do it, couldn't you?" Patty was supposed to be the innkeeper's wife; she wasn't very good, actually, but she was very pretty and did look the part, even if she was mostly looking petrified now.

"... No, Miss..." A mouse could have made more noise, and this was as loud as Patty ever spoke.

"I beg your pardon, Patty?" Nell smiled kindly at the child, rather wishing to shake her.

"She said no, Miss, and please, Miss, why is the angel Gabriel a girl? Because Gabriel is a boy's name, Miss. If it was a girl, it should be called Gabrielle, Miss, and I ha'n't never heard of the Angel Gabrielle, Miss, so it stands to reason that the angel is a boy, Miss, what with him being called Gabriel and not Gabrielle. If it's a girl angel, how come it's got a boy's name?"

Nell was rather floored by this logic, but rallied with an effort. "Gabriel can be a boy's name, yes Michael, but it is also a girl's name."

"But it can be a boy's name, Miss? So the angel mighta bin a boy, Miss?"

The boy was persistent, she'd give him that. "The angel might have been a boy, yes, but he was a girl. SHE...was a girl." Nell gave herself a shake. "Emma, what about you? I'm sure Abigail could carry the Baby Jesus up the aisle on her own?"

"No thanks, Miss." Emma pulled a face. "I don't want all them words and songs and that, I only wanted to be an angel 'cos of the wings and the tinsel. Anyhow Abigail holds the Baby Jesus all wrong if I'm not there."

"Do not!" Abigail was outraged.

"Do so, Abigail. Anyway, like Michael said, if Gabriel can be a boy, why can't the Angel Gabriel be a boy?"

"Yeah, how come, Miss, was there a rule for Angels that they had to have boy's names or something?" Michael asked. "'Cos I know that there was an Archangel Michael, like a boss of all the other angels, and he had a boy's name but they never said that he was a girl 'cos my Nan said I was named after him, Miss, and I don't think they would have named me after a girl, so if Michael was an angel who was a boy, then I don't see why Gabriel was a girl, Miss."

"Anyway, if Michael is already an angel, Miss, then he ought to be an angel, oughtn't he?" Emma went on with the inexorable logic of the young.

"Yeah, Miss!"

"Yes!"

"Michael can't be the Angel Gabriel because we need someone who would fit Suzanna's costume and Michael is much taller than Suzanna!" Nell was conscious she was fighting a losing action, but for two glorious seconds, she thought she'd settled the matter; and then Patty piped up in the biggest voice that Nell had yet heard her use.

"But, Miss, he doesn't need to fit Suzanna's costume. She'll be back by then. He's only being the Angel in the practices."

It was checkmate. There was no coming back from that.

"Can I, Miss, please, Miss, can I? I know the words and everything, listen—"I AM the Angel Gabriel!"—see?"

Nell gave up. "Very well, Michael, yes, if you want to, you can stand in for Suzanna."

"Yesss!" He punched the air, then looked a little embarrassed and lodged his hands firmly in his pockets.

Mrs. Troyd stalked over, calling over her shoulder, "Yes, Maria, but I do think that the Three Kings need to have cloaks that coordinate with the jewels on their crowns. We must be able to find a teal cloak somewhere—I have the utmost confidence with you. You have until Thursday, which I would have thought would be plenty of time. Now, Nell, have you sorted out our volunteer Angel then? Patty?"

Nell opened her mouth but Michael got there first.

"No, Mrs. T, I'm doing it! 'I AM the Angel Gabriel', see, what with Gabriel being a boy's name and everything."

Mrs. Troyd laughed shrilly. "Don't be silly, Michael, the Angel Gabriel is..." Her voiced trailed away as she saw Nell's face. "Nell...!"

"As the children pointed out, Mrs. Troyd, Gabriel is a boy's name and it is only for the practices..." Nell smiled weakly.

"Well!" Mrs. Troyd floundered for a moment. "Goodness me, that was not what I was expecting at all, but I suppose if no one else wants to do it...?" She left the question hanging hopefully for a moment, but it was met with a chorus of:

"No, Miss."

"Not me, Miss."

"Miss, Michael wants to do it, Miss!"

"Are those the words, Miss?" Michael snatched the papers out of her hand, and announced, "I AM the Angel Gabriel!"

"Yes, we know you know that bit, Michael," Nell muttered.

"Well, we shall take it under advisement." Mrs. Troyd stared daggers at her hapless colleague, who withered under that dread glare.

"What does that mean, Miss, advisement?" Michael asked anxiously.

"It's one of them things on telly." Emma looked superior at having knowledge the older boy did not. "It's where they tell you to buy things."

"Nooo, stupid, that's an advertisement!" The other innkeeper, Rachel, was scornful.

"That's what I said!" Emma's voice rose in outrage.

"Is not!"

"Is so!"

"Is not!"

"CHILDREN!" They all fell silent. You had to admire Mrs. Troyd's sheer volume, Nell thought; it did the job. "We are in church, and that means we are respectful in the presence of the Lord and do not argue about advertisements on the telly! Michael, I am afraid that I don't think you ought to do it—"

"Awwwwww, Miss!"

"—but I will talk to you at the end of the practice. For now, we do not need the Angel because we are going to run through the scene with the Mary, and Joseph, and the Donkey, and the Innkeepers! Everyone to their places, please, as we will be starting in ten seconds precisely!"

THE INNKEEPER'S SONG

The children scattered, the characters in question to the raised area of the altar and the rest to the benches where they had realised that, if they were quiet, they could play at all sorts of entertaining things.

"Right! We will start from the end of the Donkey's song!" Mrs. Troyd announced.

Joseph, who was playing the Donkey, stepped forward.

"I am very tired. I am only a little donkey and I have been carrying Mary all the way from Bethlehem. Mary has to ride on my back because she is pregnant—"

"—up the duff—" Mrs. Troyd ignored the murmur from the other side of the stage.

"—and her baby is due very soon. At last we have come to Jerusalem. I hope there will be room for us in one of the inns here." The Donkey stepped back and Joseph , played by Steven, stepped forward.

"What a long journey that was…"

"Joseph, I can't hear a word you're saying!" Mrs. Troyd stood up.

"Me, Miss?" The Donkey looked puzzled.

"No, Joseph, I meant the character Joseph, not you." She turned to Steven. "I've told you, Steven, you need to shout right out so the people at the back of the church can hear you. I'm sitting on the front row and I can hardly hear you at all. Try again, but shout this time."

"What a long journey that was…"

"No no no! Do you think that is shouting? That's no different!" She fixed him with a steely eye.

"'m sorry, Miss…"

Steven was clearly a nervous wreck, and Nell stepped forward to Mrs. Troyd's shoulder. "He's been that quiet the whole time, Mrs. Troyd. We'll have the microphone for the angels to sing into —if we get him to stand near it, it should pick up his voice. The more he thinks about it, the quieter he gets, you see."

"You may be right, Nell. Joseph, do you see the broom handle sticking up at the front of the stage here?"

"Me, Miss?"

"No, Joseph, I was still talking to Steven."

"But, Miss, Steven's called Steven and you keep saying Joseph, Miss."

"Joseph—"

"Yes, Miss?" both boys replied together.

Mrs. Troyd gritted her teeth. "Right, when I wish to speak to you, Steven Ramsbottom, I will refer to you as Steven, and when I wish to talk to you, Joseph Willikins, I will refer to you as the Donkey."

"That's not very nice, Miss, my mum says we're not supposed to call people names."

"It is NOT calling names, Joseph, because the character you are playing in the course of this nativity play IS A DONKEY! Now that's the last we'll hear of it! Right, Joseph—I mean Steven! Do you see this broom handle?"

Steven, now thoroughly intimidated, was barely audible by now. "…Yes, miss…"

"This broom handle shows where the microphone will be on the day of the play. When it's your turn to speak, I want you to come right forward and speak into the microphone. Do you understand?"

Steven thought about this, then marched forward and leant down to the broom handle. "Yes, Miss!"

"Very good. Now if you do that on the night, you'll do very well." Mrs. Troyd resumed her seat, gathering her floral skirts out of the way. "Now carry on, from 'What a long journey that was'."

"What a long journey that was! I am very tired from walking all that way, and I am worried about poor Mary, who is near her time!" Steven remembered his gesture and pointed behind him, bashing Mary on the arm. She whacked him back and he opened his mouth to object but, catching Mrs Troyd's eye, thought better of it and went on with his lines. "If we do not get a room in the inn, it will be very difficult! Here is an inn, I wonder if they have any rooms left." He banged on the wooden chair that was set to the side. "Knock knock!"

"Steven, you don't have to say 'knock knock' when you knock on the chair!" Mrs. Troyd pointed out.

Steven looked mutinous. "But, Miss, it says it in the script, Miss, and I learnt it like it said—"

"That was a stage direction dear. It says it in the script so you know to do the action, but we won't be saying it out loud any more, will we?" She glared at him.

"No, Miss." Receiving the nod, he went on. "Knock knock— sorry miss, I meant…" and he knocked on the chair.

Rachel, who was playing the first Innkeeper, stepped forward. "What do you want?"

"I want a room for the night. My wife is heavy with child and we have nowhere to stay."

"Well, you can't stay here—there's no room at the inn!" She snarled with evident relish at having the punch line.

"Rachel, dear, a bit less vicious, please. You don't dislike Joseph and Mary; it is simply that other people are already using all the rooms."

"But I like that line, Miss!" Rachel objected.

Mrs. Troyd glared at her. "Nevertheless, Rachel, a little more matter of fact, if you would."

Rachel was disgusted by this, but dutifully intoned the line expressionlessly. "You can't stay here; there is no room at the inn."

"Not that matter of fact, Rachel; something between the two." Rachel rolled her eyes with all the exasperation that a six year old can muster, while Mrs. Troyd nodded to Steven, who turned around and went over to Michael, knocking on the wooden chair over at the other side of the stage. "Knock knock—oh no, sorry, Miss, I'll get it right tomorrow."

"What do you want?" Michael grumped expressionlessly.

"Come on, Michael, you can do it better than that!"

"...Don't want to be the innkeeper, want to be the Angel Gabriel..."

"The Angel Gabriel is a girl and you are a boy and we need you to be the innkeeper!" Mrs. Troyd retorted sharply. "Now let's have enough of this nonsense and get on with the scene!" She nodded to Steven, who bent and knocked the chair again.

"Knock knock."

"What do you want?"

"My wife is heavy with child and we need a room for the night. Have you got a room for us?"

Michael opened his mouth, and then hesitated. A beatific smile spread over his face, and with a sinking feeling, Nell realised just what was coming next.

"Yes, there's plenty of room, do come in. Do you want two rooms? You can have two each if you want. We've got loads."

Steven gaped, and for three beats, so did everyone else; and then, inexorably, every pair of eyes in the room slid around to settle on Mrs. Troyd, who had gone purple to the first immaculately set wave in her iron-grey hair. She took a deep breath; and another; and then she said through gritted teeth "That's not the line, Michael, try again."

"Isn't it, Miss? I thought it was. I'm sure that was what was written on my script," he replied with a studied air of innocence. "But then it's a funny thing, Miss; them old lines for the Innkeeper, I can't remember them at all, but I know every single one for the Angel Gabriel."

There was the sort of silence that prickled like pins.

"Is that so?" Mrs Troyd's face was thunderous.

"Oh yes, miss—'I AM the Angel Gabriel', see? No problem. But that ole line for the innkeeper, well, I just can't remember that at all. I don't want to be the Innkeeper 'cos I don't want to get it wrong, see? That's why I want to be the Angel Gabriel."

Nell was almost tempted to look around in case tumbleweeds were rolling across the aisle behind her, but could not tear her gaze away from the spectacle of a nine-year-old boy besting the fearsome Mrs. Troyd.

"Right." The teacher's voice was falsely cheerful. "Right. I think that will do for today, children. You've all worked very hard. The next practice will be—what is it, Patty?"

"Please, Miss, mmmmm," the child muttered.

"Say it again, Patty, but louder." Mrs. Troyd's tone was fierce and Patty subsided. "Very well then, the next practice will be—"

"Please miss, I didn't say my line!" Patty yelled. This was as loud as she had ever been, Nell noted, wondering if she could persuade her to yell like that for the night of the play.

"Very well, Patty, you may say your line!" Mrs. Troyd snapped, and in the adrenaline rush of having made herself heard, Patty did so.

"JEBEDIAH, DON'T YOU TURN AWAY THAT POOR GIRL, SHE IS GOING TO HAVE A BABY! DON'T WORRY DEAR YOU CAN STAY IN OUR STABLE!"

"Good grief!" Nell exclaimed into the astonished silence that followed. "Patty, that was wonderful. Do you think you can say it that loud tomorrow?"

"I THINK SO, MISS!" Patty looked as surprised as anyone else, but very pleased as Nell made a great fuss of her.

"We will practice again next Thursday at six o'clock! Do not be late!" Mrs. Troyd snapped, thrust the spare script at Nell, donned her coat, and flounced out, flicking her paisley scarf around her neck with such venom that Nell could have sworn there were little whip-cracking sounds from the tassels.

"Can we go home now, Miss?" asked Rachel.

"I think so, dear. Who is waiting for their parents to come back and collect them?" Nell started to round up all the children, parcel them up into the correct coats and scarves, and send them on their way. Although the practice had finished early, most of the parents not already there arrived while she was packing up, and eventually when everything was done, there was only Michael left.

"What time is your Dad coming to pick you up, dear?" Nell smiled at him.

"Any minute, Miss; he says he doesn't like to come too soon because he can't stand that old harpy, which is weird miss, because we haven't got a harpy." He looked oddly at Nell, who had snorted involuntarily. "Do you think he means the piano, miss? That's the only musical instrument in church, Miss. Unless they have it in a cupboard or something. "

"Yes, Michael." Nell managed to keep her voice level only by a feat of self-control. "You may be right."

"Thought so." He nodded to himself with all the satisfaction of one who has put to bed a long-running mystery. "Can we go through my lines miss?"

"Certainly, dear." Nell took the outstretched papers and began. "Goodness me, what is that light that is shining through my window?"

Michael smiled beatifically.

"I AM the Angel Gabriel, and I bring you news of greaaaaat joy."

* * *

TRUE TO HIS WORD, Michael was exceedingly good as the Angel Gabriel. His parents were initially slightly baffled, but when Nell explained how persistent Michael had been, Mike Hill shook his head thoughtful and gave his slow chuckle.

"Aye, that sounds like our lad all right; he allus did know what 'e wanted and it never were quite what we expected. Did 'e say why 'e wanted to be an angel?"

"Well,." Nell did not quite know how to break this to the boy's father but could not bring herself to lie. "He seemed to be very taken by the idea of tinsel and wings."

Mr. Hill's eyebrows rose halfway to his hairline and stayed there for some moments before he reacted, then he just shrugged. "That lad! What is 'e like?! Still, 'e'll 'ear about it at school I 'ave no doubt, and if it don't vex 'im I 'ave no idea why it should vex me. 'E'll grow out of it or 'e won't; and there in't no point makin 'im feel bad about it till 'e decides one way or t'other."

"Very wise." Nell smiled with genuine warmth; she liked Mike Hill, a steady, gentle man who revelled in his family but did not particularly feel the need to lay any expectations on them.

"Besides." Mike grinned mischievously. "I'll bet 'Er 'Ighness don't like it above 'alf!"

"Er, no, I don't think she does, as you say, like it above half," Nell stammered before realising that this was possibly rather indiscreet. "Oh! I don't mean any disservice to Michael of course—"

"Don't you worry, lass, I'll never tell! Your secret is safe with me!" He tapped one broad finger along the side of his nose and winked at her, then began to fish out his car keys prior to leaving.

"Oh, Mike." Nell laid a hand on his arm, stopping him as he turned to go.

"Aye, lass?"

Nell chose her words with care. "Michael seems to be under the impression that a harpy is a musical instrument. He thinks it may be stored in a cupboard somewhere round the back. I didn't necessarily see the need to enlighten him." She looked at his horrified face and grinned in a most unladylike manner, tapping one finger along the side of her nose. "Don't you worry, Mike—your secret is safe with me!"

She left him roaring with laughter and hurried off, somewhat flustered at her own forwardness. What would her father have said? Though actually, when she thought back, her father would probably have been laughing just as hard as Mike was doing.

IT CAME UPON A MIDNIGHT CLEAR

*T*he practices went on in their own inimitable fashion and soon it was time for the dress rehearsal. The children filed in by ones and twos and the atmosphere in the church was thick with chatter and colourful with cloaks and tea towels and the odd prop.

"Right, children! Have you all got your costumes on?" Nell called, clapping her hands for order. "Then go line up along the stage and let's see how they fit."

The children lined up as if on parade and Mrs. Troyd stalked along the line with the air of a Major General inspecting the troops, Maria Effle following in her wake with a pencil and paper. "Jenny; white dress, dark blue head-dress, very good. Mary is fine, you can tick her off the list. Now where's Joseph?"

"Here, Miss!" two voices chorused.

"Where is Steven who is playing Joseph? Very good, Steven, let's see." Steven stepped forward in a square brown sack-looking thing with a dressing gown cord wrapped round him, and Mrs. Troyd eyed him critically. "Very good, Steven—where is your headdress?"

"Please, Miss, do I have to wear it, Miss? It makes my ears itch."

"Yes, Steven, you do need to wear it." Mrs. Troyd snatched the tea towel from him and jammed it on his head with the aid of an overlarge elastic band. "Maria, tick Joseph off the list. Angel Gabriel?"

"Here miss!" Michael's voice was drowned out by the grandiose entrance of Arianna le Grand and family from the back of the church.

"We are here, do not worry—the le Grands are back and the play may go on!"

"Did someone call for the Angel Gabriel?" Suzanna really did have shades of the Shirley Temple, Nell thought, watching the blonde child skip theatrically up the aisle and strike a pose in front of Mrs. Troyd. "I am here and ready for my costume!"

The children all stared.

"Suzanna, you have the strangest markings on your face." Mrs Troyd's voice was slightly stunned, matching the look on her face.

"Oh, yes, Mrs. Troyd, it's a skier's tan. Mummy says only the best skiers get them." Suzanna beamed proudly. "That's what happens when all the sun reflects on your face and you've got goggles on."

"Pity we aren't doin' Noah's Ark; then she could be a panda!" Steven's comment was intended to be quiet but carried alarmingly well in the acoustics of the church. Nell's lips twitched before she got back her face under control.

There was a rattle from the back of the church. "Alexander! Have you had an accident?" Mrs. Troyd's tones swooped towards what Nell liked to think of as Tragedy Queen depth of timbre.

"Alex fell over on the nursery slopes and broke his leg, poor baby," Arianna interjected, "but I've told him that I'm sure you wouldn't object if he sits on the side and just reads his lines in."

"You did, did you?" Nell could see the tensing of Mrs. Troyd's muscles as she gritted her teeth behind that terrible smile of hers. "Well, we'll have to take that under advisement, I'm afraid."

"Under advisement?" Arianna bristled.

"Oooh! Oooh! I know that one Mrs. Grand! It's one of them things on the telly what means you have to buy things," Emma offered, unwarily averting the wrath of Arianna onto her own head.

"LE Grand, child, it is LE Grand!"

"Oh okay." Emma was a bit taken aback but shrugged to herself, repeating dutifully, "I know that one LE Grand."

It was the last straw. With a contemptuous flick of her faux fur coat, Arianna tossed her blonde hair over her shoulder and stalked out. Mrs. Troyd watched her, allowing herself only the tiniest of smirks, but this quickly faded when she turned back to the altar to find Suzanna squaring up with Michael.

"Er, Mrs. Troyd?" Suzanna ventured delicately. "Why is this boy wearing wings?"

"I AM the Angel Gabriel!" Michael was defiant before the slightly panda-faced but rather more overtly angelic form before him.

"But you can't be the Angel Gabriel, because you see, I am." Suzanna's tone was sweetly reasonable. "And besides, you're a boy, and I'm a girl, and I have blonde hair and I look right. You're a big clumsy boy, and you haven't even got blonde hair. So you see, you can't be the Angel Gabriel because everyone knows that angels are girls."

"Gabriel can too be a boy." Michael was downcast but not yet beaten. "Like the Archangel Michael was a boy. I can too be the Angel Gabriel."

"Don't be silly, of course you can't." Suzanna was clearly channelling her mother, Nell thought as she hurried across. "You would look silly—a boy in a dress? Are you weird or something? Boys don't wear dresses."

Nell drew a sharp breath, and just as she was formulating the words to stop this bitchy little tirade, Michael did it for her.

"Yeah, really weird, when ALL the costumes are dresses. Dun't matter if you're a Shepherd or a King or an Innkeeper, there in't any trousers in this play. The only one what dun't wear a dress is the Baby Jesus and he's just got a tea towel on."

Suzanna was floored by this for a moment before her persistent nature won through. "Yes, but the girls ALWAYS get the wings and the tinsel and the pretty things."

"They don't get all the pretty things though, do they?" Michael put his head on one side. "I mean, if you was the Angel Gabriel, you'd have to wear this borin' ole white dress. Looks like they made it from an ole bed sheet and it han't even got any good patterns on it anyhow. Tell you what, you can 'ave it, an' these daft ole wings and the tinsel too, if you want. I just thought that, what with you bein' a girl an' girls liking colours an' that, it might be better if I had the borin' dress. But if you 'ave it, that means I can have the other one, and that's better anyhow." He turned as if to go, but Suzanna stopped him.

"What other one? I don't want your brown innkeeper dress."

Michael looked away loftily. "Not the innkeeper dress, the big green cloak what the King wears, an' the shiny crown too, that's what I thought you might like but you already bin on holiday an' stuff so you don't need a treat. Tell you what, you have the angel dress an' I'll be the king, right?"

"But there already are three kings," Suzanna protested, "and you can't have four."

"Yes, but your Alex dun't want to be in it, does he?" Michael turned to Alex. "If it was me what had a broken leg an' a pot an' everything, I'd be sittin' in front of the telly watchin' Power Monkeys Christmas Special an' eatin' chocolate, not sittin' in some ole church bein' the King of Skiing for a play."

This was a shrewd blow in several respects.

"The King of Skiing?" Alex wrinkled his nose anxiously. Having caused him quite as much discomfort and ridicule as it had (especially from his loving twin), skiing was not his favourite pastime at the moment, whereas watching the Power Monkeys

Christmas Special with chocolate seemed by comparison a quite acceptable option.

"Really, the King of Skiing?" Having brought Suzanna nothing but praise and plaudits, on the other hand, skiing was her new love and the thought of anyone else being the skier in the play burned at her competitive little soul.

"Oh yes," Michael continued with the same lack of interest. "They was thinking they'd have to draw on them marks on their faces what you've got already, which is why I thought you'd want to do it, what with you being a real skier an' all, but seein' as you want the white dress—"

"Michael, I've been thinking that, really, seeing as how Alex doesn't want to be the King and you have done all the practises being the Angel, that it would be kinder of me to be the King instead of Alex so that you can be the Angel Gabriel." Suzanna's voice dripped with sugary goodwill. Alex looked a bit startled at this as he had not actually made the decision to drop out yet, but the lure of the Power Monkeys was strong, especially with the addition of chocolate.

Michael pulled a face, though. "Well, I dunno... I mean, it's a really boring' dress an' all."

"Oh please, Michael!" Suzanna pleaded, dropping all pretence of altruism. "Go on, I was the Angel last year AND the year before that and I want a go with the green cloak and the shiny crown! I'll be your best friend!"

"You will not, you're a girl!"

Michael was quite indignant at this so Suzanna took another tack. "I'll give you a chocolate bar..."

"You han't got one."

"I have too! It's a foreign one too, from France. I bought it on holiday and I was going to give it to Mrs. Troyd, but you can have it instead. But you have to be the Angel, because I want to be the King of Skiing."

Michael considered this for a moment, before agreeing with

every appearance of exasperation. "Oh all right then, I'll be the Angel…"

Suzanna ran away, beaming, to get the chocolate bar quick before he could change his mind. Michael looked across at Alex.

"Which one's your favourite Power Monkey, then?" Alex ventured cautiously.

"ZapApe. What's yours?"

"ElectroMonkey, I think, though ZapApe is pretty cool," Alex conceded. "I don't like ShockOrang though, he's really annoying."

"Too right." Michael nodded. "So in a fight between Spiderman and ElectroMonkey, who do you reckon would win?"

"Here!" Suzanna returned, thrusting a substantial bar of chocolate under Michael's nose. "But you absolutely have to be the Angel, right?"

"Right." Michael took the chocolate and they watched her skip off, ringlets bouncing. "So—Spiderman or ElectroMonkey?"

OVER BY THE ALTAR, Jenny Clark was holding court. She was dressed in her Mary costume but on her feet, she was wearing searingly pink rollerboots with silver flashes along the side. These were causing something of a stir amongst the other girls, which Jenny was clearly enjoying.

"My Granny gave them to me for Christmas. I've got a pink helmet an' a pink kneepad anna nother pink kneepad anna pink glove thing anna nother pink glove thing anna—"

"How come you opened 'em already if it's a Christmas present?" Daisy was awed at this concession.

"My Granny said I could. My Granny gives me lots of things and she always lets me open them when I want to."

The other children considered this.

"What sort of things?" Lucy Melcombe, the Second King, had all the suspicion of a child three years older than Jenny.

"All sorts of things."

"Like what though?"

Jenny frowned. "Like lots of things, silly!" But sensing that this would not do, she went on, "Like... like a bike anna Bratz doll anna Harry Potter wand an' Power Monkeys pyjamas anna puppy anna—"

"You han't got a puppy though," objected Lucy, who was on reasonably good terms with Jenny's older sister, "so that in't true for starters, she din't give you a puppy."

"I din't say she gave me a puppy!" Jenny affected outrage at this.

"Did too!"

"Did not, I said she give me things like a puppy an' all that!" Jenny was flustered and a little bit cross by now and it wasn't helped by the fact that just at that moment Rachel came to see what she was up to.

"JEN! Are you wearing them rollerboots in church?! Mum's gonna kill you, you know you weren't even supposed to know we had them. You're such a little sneak sometimes!"

This resulted in two seconds of delighted silence amongst the others.

"Thought she was give them by your Nan, Rachel? Thought she was allowed to open 'em early an' everything?" Lucy grinned maliciously; she could be a real troublemaker at times, and this was one of them.

Rachel turned to Jenny. "Just you wait till I tell our Mum on you! Fibbing in church, and you the Virgin Mary and everything! If you think Santa's visiting you this year, you're gonna be sad on Christmas morning!"

Much upset, Jen jumped to her feet, wobbled on the rollerboots and caught herself on a pew. "Ha! You must be some sort of baby if you think Santa comes to visit you! I've seen Mum an' Dad bringin' in the presents! If you think you're getting a visit from

Santa you're gonna be sad too, only I got Barbie pink rollerboots and you han't!" With which Parthian shot, she made a valiant effort to flounce off, but not having quite got the hang of the rollerboots, she ended up doing a strange kind of forward shuffle down the aisle, pulling herself along the arms of the pews—but with added flounce.

"What does that mean, Rachel?" Abigail asked. "Why does your Mum an' Dad bring the presents in an' not Santa?"

"Doesn't Santa come to your house then?" Little Daisy was soft-hearted enough that this made tears come to her eyes.

Rachel, staring down in horror at the trusting eyes of the little Brett girls, was conscious of an abyss opening before her feet. Lucy was no help at all as, sensing trouble, she suddenly needed to go talk to Suzanna.

"No, Santa doesn't come in the house," Rachel stammered, and then had a flash of inspiration. "I mean, of course he comes into the garden an' that, an' Rudolph an' his sleigh an' all, but he dun't come inside the house any more. We han't got a chimney so he has to knock on the door."

"Do you put out mince pies for him, and that?" Patty chimed in.

"Well, we used to, but that's why he won't come in, see..." Rachel gazed down the aisle at the receding rollerboots and added with relish, "...'cos last year Jen ate the mince pies and put some Brussels sprout pies there instead."

"Brussels sprout pies?! Yuck!" the girls chorused.

"Yeah, they was gross and Santa ate them and he puked up everywhere, and it smelt of Brussels sprouts, and my Mum had to clean it all up an' now she won't let him in again." Rachel assumed a rather superior look at this success. "So he comes an' knocks on the door and Mum and Dad bring in the Christmas presents and put them under the tree an' that."

"Gosh!" Patty and Abigail exchanged looks of awe.

"That's all she meant, yeah? Anyhow, where did Lizzie go?" Feeling she had extricated herself honourably, Rachel walked off to tell her friend Lizzie about the troublemaking qualities of younger sisters.

THE GREATEST GIFT OF ALL

*M*rs. Troyd, meanwhile, had finished checking her way through the costumes and, having satisfied herself that the various props were listed and to hand, was now ready to start the rehearsal.

Eleanor, who was playing the First King, had also been given the opening introduction and was reading this in full costume. Suzanna watched jealously; being the First King, Eleanor had a shiny red cloak and a crown with glittering red jewels. Suzanna would have liked to swap the green ones Alex had been given for these ruby jewels, but she had no illusions of being able to persuade the older girl to do it, and still had in front of her the mammoth task of persuading Mrs. Troyd to allow the change of roles she had in mind.

"Very good, Eleanor, but tomorrow night you mustn't forget to leave your King costume on the bench when you're being the narrator or it will look very odd." Mrs. Troyd gestured the girl to return to her seat. "Now, Mary and Gabriel, are you ready? Michael, now that Suzanna's back, she'll be playing the Angel so you don't need to."

"Please, Mrs. Troyd, I'd rather Michael did it," Suzanna's voice echoed across the church. "I was the Angel last year and the year before and I think it's someone else's turn now." Mrs. Troyd being clearly unconvinced by this statement, Suzanna glanced at Michael, who nodded at her meaningfully. She smiled sweetly and deployed the line he had given her. "Of course, I will if you'd like me to Mrs. Troyd, but the thing is, after all the fun we had on holiday, I'm not sure I'll remember the lines."

"What?!" No fool, Mrs. Troyd had seen—and was reasonably sure she understood—the look, but the concept of Suzanna le Grand being in cahoots with Michael Hill was too alien to even consider.

"Well, we were having such fun that we didn't really look at them much. It's such a long time since we went to a practice, and seeing as Michael's done all the rehearsals, it just seems like a much better idea for him to be the Angel, Miss." Suzanna wore such an air of sincerity and innocence that Mrs. Troyd could not bring herself to doubt the girl. Besides, it was so like Suzanna to make such a sacrifice for the good of the play, she thought, and beamed at her.

"I know all the lines and everything, Miss—'I AM the—'"

"Yes, I know you know them, Michael," Mrs. Troyd returned testily. "And it would seem that, as you have been to all the practices and as Suzanna would prefer it and as Mrs. Effle seems to have made the costume to fit you rather than Suzanna—" She paused to stare daggers at that hapless lady before finishing with heavy resignation, "Then, yes, you may take the part of the Angel Gabriel."

"Yesss!" Michael punched the air again, looking smug.

"Well then. Shall we go through your scene with Mary?"

"Yes, Miss, I'm all ready and everything, Miss." Michael went to stand at the side of the stage where he was due to enter.

"Jenny? Where is Jenny?"

"Here, Miss!" Jenny rollerbooted up the aisle and onto the altar.

"What on earth...?" Mrs. Troyd knew better than to pursue that course of investigation and settled for merely grinding her teeth. "Jenny, go and put on some proper shoes at once! You can't wear rollerboots on the altar!"

"Why not, Miss, does Jesus not like rollerboots?" Jenny was genuinely interested by this.

"Not when they was opened when Mum particularly said not to look in the bag."

Mrs. Troyd ignored the murmur from the pews. "No, Jenny, they are not appropriate for a church and you might fall over and hurt yourself. Now go and change them!"

"But, Miss, I han't got any other boots here," Jenny objected and for a moment it seemed there might be trouble, but Mrs. Troyd glanced at her watch and shook her head.

"We haven't got time for this nonsense now, but be warned, Jenny, if you turn up with rollerboots tonight, there will be Trouble!"

"Yes, Miss." Jenny hung her head, but was gestured to take her place. Rolling over to the altar, she knelt down with some difficulty, joined her hands in prayer and assumed a pious expression

A FEW ROWS BACK, Suzanna was plotting with Lucy Melcombe, the Second King, and the other children were variously whispering or playing. Alex sat trying to scratch his leg under the plaster with a ruler. A shy child, overshadowed by his overconfident sister, he had few friends but was now watching Michael somewhat speculatively as a fellow Power Monkeys enthusiast and potential saviour from the doom of being a picturesque but ultimately pointless Third King.

"But when they're in the stable, right, and there's Mary an' Joseph an' the shepherds an' that," Patty whispered, "them three kings turn up with presents, right?"

"Yeah." Emma was not at all sure where this was going but it was an interesting line of enquiry.

"An' the presents is called gold, Frankenstein, and myrrh, right? Well, why do they give that to a baby?"

They considered this.

"Well the gold, that might be a bracelet or spoon or something," Emma ventured. "We went to a christening and everyone give presents to the baby and it was all like spoons and metal teddy bears an' that. Maybe the gold is like a christening present."

"Not a Christmas present then?"

Emma looked thoughtful. "Maybe they said to 'im 'Bring a Christmas present' and 'e just 'eard it wrong."

"I bet 'e did too, my Dad's always doin' that." Patty nodded to herself. "So what about the Frankenstein?"

"Is it like a teddy but shaped like a Frankenstein?"

"Looks like a box to me."

"Maybe that's the box it comes in, like a Barbie or summat."

"Ohhhh. What's myrrh?"

Emma, proud of her role as source of all wisdom, did not have a clue what myrrh was but was reluctant to admit it. "It's biscuits," she told them. "Like with spices in an' currants an' that."

"Is there chocolate ones in it?" Abigail was not at all sure about currants.

"No, just spices an' currants an' that." Emma had a few qualms about making it up in church, but consoled herself with the fact that there definitely were some biscuits like that, and they might very well actually be called myrrh biscuits for all she knew, so if it wasn't right, how was she to know?

"In't that a bit rubbish presents for a baby?" Patty wrinkled her brow in an effort to remember. "We bought some presents for Jason's baby an' we got it a rattle and a—y'know, one of them baby suits. We din't get it some biscuits an' a spoon an' a Frankenstein."

"Maybe it's like rusks. Babies eat rusks," Abigail offered.

"I would ha' thought," Emma interrupted, "that they would've got something proper, not some rusks an' a Frankenstein an' an ole spoon. I mean, Jesus dun' even have a rattle or a dummy or anything. I bet Mary and Joseph was sittin' there sayin' 'Where's his dummy? He dun't have one', an' that, and Jesus in a manga and everything."

"In't it a manger? I thought it was a baby in a manger."

"No, it's a manga." Emma assumed an air of lofty superiority.

"'Tis not!"

"'Tis so!"

"'Tis not!"

"All right then, you tell me, what is a manger then? Bet you don't know, do you, 'cos it's not a manger, it's a manga!"

Patty looked at the stage uncertainly. "In't it kind of a box? When you bring on the Baby Jesus an' 'e's in the stable, you put 'im in a box. I thought that were the manger."

"Nooooo silly, that's a crib. You put babies in a crib, not in a manger."

"So what's a manga then?" Abigail was entirely confused now.

"It's like cartoons, but with karate and kung fu, and they all talk funny and fly and that." Emma nodded knowledgeably, but Patty was not necessarily convinced.

"Wait a minute, when was Jesus in a cartoon? 'Cos I han't seen it."

"Noooooo silly, it was ages ago, when he was growin' up an' that." Emma rolled her eyes. "It was when he was twelve an' he went to Jerusalem and they learned him karate and flyin' and 'e was in a cartoon."

"But he was real, wan't he? Real people don't go in cartoons."

"What about Jackie Chan then? Jackie Chan was in cartoons and he was in films too so he must have been a real person. And he did flying and karate and that."

"Girls! Quiet there please! We're trying to rehearse!" Mrs. Troyd called and the three of them jumped guiltily and sat still until she turned back to the altar.

Then Patty shrugged. It was true, she had seen the cartoons and everything. "Alright then, maybe it is."

Emma gave her a smug look, but Mrs. Troyd turned round again, and so she let it drop.

WHEN IT GOT to the three Kings, Suzanna appeared in the place of Alex, and though at first indignant that this was the case, Mrs. Troyd quickly saw the advantages of the situation. After all, it wasn't as if Alex had had any lines, poor dear, because he was too shy to say them, so all Suzanna had to do was to put on the cloak and crown, follow the others, and say, "And myrrh for sadness," which was well within her skill set. Mrs. Troyd knew she shouldn't have favourites but was quite pleased the poor girl was getting to be in the play after all, as she enjoyed it so every year.

Suzanna played her part immaculately in rehearsal, but she had not realised just how little was involved when she agreed to take the part and felt that she had been duped, so she took her cloak and crown and returned to her seat pensively to consider what was the best way of remedying this.

EVENTUALLY THE REHEARSAL drew to a close and the parents turned up again. Stephanie Grant burst into tears when she saw her mother and was whisked off. Jenny Clark got a good telling-off from her mother for the rollerboots, not least as that harassed lady had to deal with Rachel waxing lyrical on how Jenny had lied about it so that Jenny ended up also bursting into tears and flouncing off again to the best of her ability on the lurid pink wheels. Lizzie Willikins and Lucy Melcombe appeared from the back room in sparkly jeans and excruciatingly fashionable matching tops, their hair in vertical ponytails on the tops of their heads, and stood posing at the side of the church until Mrs. Melcombe turned up to take them to their party. Joseph Willikins was not going to the party with his sister and stood, red of face and irritable, until his lift appeared. One by one, the other parents appeared, promised faithfully to deliver child and costume back to the church on time, and disappeared, leaving only Mrs. Troyd, Nell, and Maria Effle behind them.

"Goodness, what a terrible practice!" Mrs. Troyd huffed.

"Dress rehearsal though." Nell had this sequence down to an art form, as it was repeated most years. "Far better to have a terrible dress rehearsal than a good one, because if it all goes well, they just relax and get sloppy. This way they have something to prove."

"That is true."

"Besides, I thought it was lovely!" Maria Effle beamed. "The children are all so good! Fair brought tears to my eyes, it did."

"That's a good point—if people don't know the play, they won't notice the mistakes," Nell added. "All we can do now is go home, have a cup of tea, and check everything's in place when we get back."

"You're very sensible, Nell." Mrs. Troyd cast a last glance around the church and grabbed her coat and bag. "I'll do just that. You have a set of keys, don't you?"

"I do." Nell took them out.

"See you this evening then!" And Mrs. Troyd swanned down the aisle, paused in the crisp pale sunlight that flooded in the door, and was gone.

"Leaving us to clear up the mess and set the place up," Maria noted acidly.

"As always, Maria!"

They grinned ruefully at each other and began to return the benches and chairs to where they needed to be at the beginning of the play.

O COME, ALL YE FAITHFUL

*H*alf past six, and chaos reigned. Nell and Maria were in the church setting up the stage with Patrick Prim, the deacon, when the church door banged open and Mrs. Troyd's voice echoed in the quiet.

"Nell! Are you there?"

Patrick rolled his eyes. "I think I'll go and dust the sacristy," he muttered, sidling off unobtrusively.

"Nell! A terrible thing has happened!" Mrs. Troyd was giving it the full Tragedy Queen as they entered the church; Nell was impressed.

"What on earth is the matter?"

"Chicken pox, Nell! The play has been assailed by chicken pox!"

Beset by a sudden vision of a spotty Nativity, Nell had to turn a guffaw into a cough. Maria was so assailed by coughing that she could barely breathe.

"Go take a glass of water, dear, do," Mrs. Troyd commanded, and as Maria made her escape, went on, "Stephanie Grant's mother rang, and she thinks that Stephanie has chicken pox so she can't be in the play. We will have to do without a sheep!"

"Oh poor little Stephanie, to be ill over Christmas! Is she very poorly with it?"

Mrs. Troyd cast a withering look at Nell. "Evidently so, or she wouldn't have dropped out of the play!"

Well, either that or Stephanie had finally persuaded her mother that she would prefer to watch the PowerMonkeys, Nell found herself thinking, and chided herself for being uncharitable. "At least she only had a couple of lines, and most of them were 'Baaa!' so we should be able to persuade one of the other children to say them. Or actually, it might be easier to just cut the lot."

"We will lose the symmetry of the stable scene entirely!" Mrs. Troyd was not to be comforted.

Nell did not grit her teeth, but contented herself with shaking her head. "Yes, what a pity."

The door banged open and Michael Hill came in with his Dad, who was carrying a large sombrero-wearing straw donkey in a fetching shade of scarlet.

"It will make the Stable Song difficult," Mrs. Troyd went on, lost in thought.

Nell dragged her gaze away from the amazing donkey with a curious sense of foreboding. "We can just ask the children to sing the whole line, maybe? They sometimes do it accidentally anyway, so instead of having Stephanie sing 'Baaa' the children all sing 'the sheep says 'Baa'—"

"That is a possibility, but it will look very odd if Daisy does her 'Moo' then."

"Oh but we can't take that off her." Nell laid a hand on Mrs Troyd's arm. "She's so proud of having something to say all on her own; she would be terribly upset."

Mrs. Troyd looked down at the hand on her arm, and Nell removed it hurriedly.

"Please, Miss?" Michael stood there with the scarlet donkey, but Mrs. Troyd spared him hardly a glance.

"Not now, Michael, we're busy!"

"But, Miss...!"

"In a moment, Michael," Nell told him kindly. "Stephanie has had to drop out and we're trying to work out what to do about her lines."

"Not just Stephanie," a voice rumbled, and Nell turned to find Michael's dad behind her. "Just had a phone call from the Willikins'. Joseph isn't well. 'Is Nan gave 'im a bag of jelly sweets, 'e ate the lot an' 'as been throwing up ever since. 'Is mum says she's ever so sorry but she 'ad to put 'im to bed an' 'e won't be able to turn up tonight."

"Yeah, Miss, so I brought me Dad's best donkey, Miss, what me Nan brung from"—Michael concentrated for a moment—"Torramaleenoes. But we thought what with Joseph not being here, Steven an' Jenny can have a donkey and then it will be all right."

Conscious that Mrs. Troyd was rummaging in her bag for what could even be smelling salts, Nell smiled weakly. "That was very thoughtful, Michael, thank you."

"You're welcome, Miss!" Michael grinned widely and took his donkey into the room round the back where the children were to change into their costumes.

Mike Hill looked a tad shamefaced. "Sorry about that, 'e would insist on bringing it. Don't feel you 'ave to use it though."

"Thank you for letting us know about Joseph, Mike." Nell gave him a genuine smile and he nodded and went to sit in his bench.

Various other children began to file in with their parents, and Nell made her excuses and went into the back room to help them all get dressed, leaving Mrs. Troyd in a state of mild collapse in the front row of the church. Maria Effle was already in there, sorting things out with her usual unflappable good humour. Michael put his donkey to one side, where the little angels were very taken with it and started petting it and calling it "horsey". He donned his tinsel and wings with every appearance of glee, and wandered round the back of the room muttering his lines.

Melanie Brett came in with the little Bretts and Rowland the dog. Patty had the lead and took the scruffy but good-humoured mutt to meet her other friends while Melanie went to find Nell.

"Nell, I thought you should know, Mr. Melcombe phoned up in a bit of a state," she confided. "He took Lizzie and Lucy to their party and his car broke down on the way back. Lizzie and Lucy are still at the party, Mr. Melcombe is stuck halfway down the bypass, and he's been waiting for the AA to turn up since half past three."

"Oh dear." Nell thought about this. "I don't suppose the Willikins' could pick them up, could they? I know Joseph's not well so someone needs to be in the house—could Mr. Willikins do it, do you think?"

Melanie shook her head. "No, he's at work until seven. He's said he'll go and pick them up as soon as he finishes work, but there's no way he can get them back in time. Lucy's dad might be able to, but only if the AA can fix his car, and as of fifteen minutes ago, they hadn't even turned up. I think you're going to have to do it without either of them."

"Oh dear. Have you told Mrs. Troyd?"

"Yes, she knows. I didn't know if you'd want to go out and discuss what to do with her, though?"

The question hung in the air for a moment in the chaos of the changing room, and then Nell twinkled at the other woman. "I think that I should probably help the children get changed. I'm sure she'll tell me when she's come up with an alternative plan—though hopefully we won't need it, of course."

Melanie laughed. "I'm sure she will. Shall I give you a hand?"

"That would be very kind."

Seven o'clock came and went. The le Grands appeared at quarter past seven, much to Mrs. Troyd's discomfort, Suzanna resplendent in a blue satin dress with a white bow and enough lace that she resembled a small steam cloud, and Alex looking very grumpy as his mother fussed about placing a large floral cushion under his leg. Arianna and Mrs. Troyd exchanged beamingly saccharine smiles. While they were exchanging the sort of pleasant but barbed small talk that ranks with a mild strafing in terms of parochial warfare, Michael took the opportunity to nip out of the back room and dashed over to talk to Alex, who was at first startled by this angelic vision but smiled in genuine welcome.

"When I thought about it, I wan't sure they'd let you stop in and watch the Christmas Special," Michael said quickly, "an' it seemed a bit mean that you'd 'ave to come and watch the play but not be in it, so I fetched you this." He handed across a crumpled bag, which Alex unfolded.

"Aw, wicked!" Alex's face lit up at sight of the PowerMonkey Christmas Fun Bag. "Can I open it now?"

"Yeah, go on! See which one you get!"

Alex pulled open the top and peered inside. "It's... oh cool, it's ElectroMonkey and everything!" He pulled out a luridly coloured plastic figurine.

"Press the button on his back," Michael grinned. "It's got ZapAttack motion an' all!"

Alex did so, and the figurine moved its arms feebly. "Cooool!"

"I'd best go, your Mum's comin' back, but there's a comic in there and a sweet and some stuff. Somethin' to do while your Suzanna's bein' the King of Skiing, huh?"

Alex grinned back with a spark of mischief that Michael hadn't often seen in him. "She has some ideas about that."

"I bet she does, an' all!" Michael sniggered, but seeing Arianna was on her way over, he scooted back to the safety of the changing room.

THE REMAINING CHILDREN all turned up (thankfully, Nell thought) and Mrs. Troyd came up with her alternative plan. Having advised all the children of the alterations, she gathered them all together into the back room for the pre-show pep-talk. "Now, children, have you all got your costumes on?"

"Yes, Mrs. Troyd!" they chorused

"—Mrs. Troyd!" Daisy was a beat behind the rest.

"Have you all checked that you have all your props?"

"Yes, Mrs. Troyd!"

"—Mrs. Troyd!"

"Right. Then everyone sit down on the floor and let's go through one or two last notes. The introduction—Eleanor, remember yours is the first voice everyone will hear so you need to speak slowly and clearly and breathe in the places we talked about."

"Yes, Miss!"

"Jenny: Mary is only a young girl and she has not read the script so do remember that when the Angel Gabriel turns up she should be surprised. She is sitting in her room and there is suddenly an Angel standing there so you can be a bit surprised and a little bit frightened, even if you like."

"Like this, Miss?" Jenny struck a highly dramatic pose.

"Not exactly like that, Jenny, but that's the general idea. Now, Joseph—,"

"He's not here, Miss!" Abigail Brett interjected.

"Steven who is playing Joseph,"—Mrs. Troyd glared at Abigail, who subsided)—"you did very well this morning but I need you to talk into the microphone more. Where the broom was this morning, that's where the microphone will be and you need to be facing straight at it so that it can pick up your voice. Can you do that, Steven?"

"Yes, Miss."

"Kings…." Mrs Troyd hesitated.

"Please, Mrs. Troyd, is it true that Lucy and Lizzie won't be back in time?" Suzanna demanded. "We can't be the Two Kings, Miss, though actually we're not Kings anyhow because Kings aren't girls but there should be three of us."

"Lizzie's dad has gone to pick the girls up from their party," Mrs. Troyd said with a smile as false as her teeth, "and we hope they will be back in time, but if it comes to it, we must start without them and the remaining two Kings will just have to act twice as hard. Do you think you can do that for me, girls?"

"Yes, Miss!" Eleanor replied glumly but Suzanna joined in with a spark in her eye that made Nell wonder if that line hadn't been something of a mistake.

"My goodness, is that the time already?!" Mrs. Troyd looked at her watch as Father Hume popped his head through the door. "Has anyone got any last questions?"

Abigail Brett put her hand up. "Please, Miss, what if we forget our words?"

"You all know the story, children; if you forget your words, just say something that means the same thing. And if the person in your scene doesn't use exactly the right words, just wait till they finish and then say your line."

"You've all worked so hard on this, children. People will enjoy it even if the words aren't quite what's written on the script. Just do the best you can." Nell got a frown from Mrs. Troyd for that interjection but it quickly turned into a gracious smile as the priest came over.

"Father, would you like to say a few words to the children?"

Father Hume turned to the motley crew of tea-towel-headed urchins before him. "Good evening, children. I know you've all worked very hard on this play and your parents will be very excited about it, but so will many of the other people in church. There are a lot of people who have no family, no parents or children or brothers and sisters, and end up spending Christmas on their own. They like to come to Mass too and they all love your Christmas play; it makes their whole Christmas. So go out there and enjoy yourselves, and make the play as good as you possibly can, not just for Mrs. Troyd and Nell here, and not just for your mums and dads, but for all those people in the church who have come here especially to see it. And when the play is over and we all go into the Parish Hall for mince pies—and I hope you're all going to have a mince pie, children?"

"Yes, Father!" a dozen voices chimed in.

"Glad to hear it! Well, then, when you go into the Parish Hall and you're scoffing all those lovely mince pies that the ladies of the parish have so kindly provided for us, just have a look around, and if you see someone sitting there on their own, or looking lonely or looking sad, just go over to them and say, "Happy Christmas," will you?"

"Yes, Father!"

"Very good! Now go out there, enjoy the play, and I'll see you afterwards." Smiling kindly at them, the priest went back into the sacristy and the children began to chatter again.

"Abigail, what are you doing dear?" Mrs. Troyd glared at the younger Brett girl who was bending underneath the bench and arguing ferociously with Emma.

"Please, Miss, my dog Rowland is a good dog, Miss, an' Emma says he looks like a sheep, Miss—"

"Did not!"

"Did too!"

"Did not!"

"—And I was thinkin', Miss, that we don't have a sheep, what with Stephanie bein' off sick, Miss, so Rowland could be like a sheep, Miss—"

"Ha! That's what you say, Miss Smartypants," Emma interrupted indignantly. "I said your dog could be a sheepdog like what my Granddad watches on the telly, that's what I said, an' 'e could be a sheepdog, couldn't 'e Miss? Rowland, Miss, 'e could be a sheepdog?"

"Yes, Emma, I'm sure he could." Mrs. Troyd was only half listening, watching a whispered conversation between Melanie Brett and Nell, presumably with news of Lizzie and Lucy's progress.

"Today, Miss, could he today? Be a dog-sheep?" Abigail sounded suddenly delighted and Mrs. Troyd smiled absently at the mixing up of the words.

"Of course he could, Abigail, any day he wants to."

"Oh wow, thanks Miss, just wait till I tell my Mum!"

"No time now, dear, we're about to start." Mrs. Troyd cleared her throat and all the children fell silent. "Right, children, have you all got everything?"

"Yes, Miss!"

"—smiss…"

"Did you leave your props in the right places, on the benches or at the side of the stage?"

"Yes, Miss!"

"—smiss…"

"Then form a line here, in the order that we told you, and we'll go in."

There were some moments of pushing and shoving, and the children got into line. Melanie Brett led one line in with Nell at the other end, and Maria Effle headed off the second. They all trooped into the church, which was filled to bursting as it was only once a year (that being the best Christmas present that anyone could have given Father Hume). After some waving and hissing of "That's my Dad up there," the children all settled, and the evening began in earnest.

LITTLE DONKEY, LITTLE DONKEY

*T*he lights dimmed.

"Remember, you're scared when you see the angel, Jenny!" Mrs. Troyd hissed.

"Yes, Miss!" Jenny put on a face of great piety and went to kneel on the stage. Michael followed her out and stood at the side.

Eleanor went to stand in the lectern and, after a moment of nervousness, took a firm hold on her script and began. "Mary was a girl who lived in Israel a long time ago. She was very pure and virtuous and God smiled on her. She was praying in her room one day when she saw a light and was amazed."

"Goodness me, what is that light that is shining through my window?"

"She turned to look and there before her stood a youth of great beauty."

This being Michael's cue, he leapt out onto the stage with rather unangelic enthusiasm, caught his trainers on the tinselled hem of his costume, and skidded to a stop.

"Who are you that appear suddenly in my chamber?" Jenny was looking nicely alarmed, though this was more because

Michael had nearly taken out the Paschal Candle and she was watching it teeter back and forth behind him.

"I AM the Angel Gabriel," he declared with great gusto.

"Aaaaaaaaaaaaaargggggghhhh oooaaaaaaaaaaaarrrrgh!" Jenny screamed. Michael jumped back in fright, setting the Paschal Candle wobbling again.

Jenny stopped, took a breath and shrieked again in a similarly dramatic fashion. "Aaaaaaaaaaaaaarrrrghhhh oooooooooohhhh—"

"'Ere, what are you doing?" Michael demanded indignantly. "It din't say in the script 'Mary screams like a great big girl,' did it?!"

"Nooo, I'm bein' scared like Mrs. Troyd tole me," Jenny's stage whisper penetrated to the back of the church. "Anyway, Mary was a great big girl."

"Well are you finished bein' scared yet? Only it's my turn."

"Nearly—ooooooooooaaaaaaaaaaaarrrrhhh oooooooooh—okay, your go."

Michael's indignant look faded, to be replaced by one of vague panic. "I've forgot me words now, see what you done!"

"I am the Angel Gabriel—" Nell prompted, and his panic turned into relief.

"I AM the Angel Gabriel and I come from God. He has decided to let his Son come into the world and he wants you to be 'is mother. Jesus's mother, anyhow." Michael was conscious that this was not quite right, but felt it was near enough.

"Yeah, all right then," Jenny shrugged, adding as the words came back to her. "Oooh no, wait, I know this one—'Let it be done to me as you have said!'"

"Okay." Michael went back to his place, Jenny got up and Steven came clacking onto the altar.

"What on earth is he wearing on his feet?" Mrs. Troyd hissed into Nell's ear. Looking up, Nell realised he was wearing football boots, complete with spikes. Silent on the carpet of the back room, here on the wooden stage they were anything but.

"You did tell them sports shoes were acceptable." Nell had to work to suppress a grin, and Mrs. Troyd sat back, indignant.

"Mary was engaged to be married to a man called Joseph," Eleanor went on. "He was very angry when he found out she was pregnant and decided he was not going to marry her; but then God sent an angel to him in a dream."

Michael walked on again, rather more cautiously this time. "God sent me to tell you to marry Mary."

Steven clacked over to the microphone and bent right over to speak into it. "WHY?" His voice boomed across the church as he clacked back into place, and various pensioners in the congregation clutched their hearing aids as they were nearly felled by the feedback.

"She has done nothing wrong and the baby she carries is God's own son, Jesus."

"My mum says every baby needs a father." Emma's voice was quiet but she was sitting near enough that the microphone picked up this comment, causing vague shiftings of amusement across the congregation.

Steven clacked over to the microphone again, and with a sea of eyes staring at him, forgot his line entirely. "S'pose so. I'd best go and marry her then." And as he clacked back off the stage, Michael stood indecisive for a moment, then shrugged and left the other side.

"Now it was the time of the census," Eleanor continued in an expressive but slightly bored tone, "and Caesar declared that everyone must go to the hometown of their House to be counted. Mary and Joseph were of the house of David, and so they had to travel all the way to Bethlehem. Mary was heavy with child."— which was to say, Jenny had stuffed a cushion up her front, although one of the corners was poking out of her front in a rather odd-looking manner. Mike Hill, in his bench, was suddenly reminded of John Hurt's famous scene in Alien, and came out with a most strange-sounding cough, quickly muffled between hand and moustache as his wife jabbed him in the ribs.

"Mary was heavy with child," Eleanor repeated loudly, "and so Joseph had bought a donkey... for... the... journey...." Her voice faltered as a wave of smirks rolled across the congregation. Individually they were barely noticeable but collectively quite disconcerting, and she glanced round to find that Steven had ducked behind the altar and reappeared with Michael's sombrero'd donkey, resplendent in scarlet and adorned—A rather nice touch, Nell thought—with a jolly tinsel hatband. He carefully placed the donkey on the stage, where it promptly fell over. Jenny straightened it again and Steven gave her the end of what looked like a dog leash, presumably borrowed from Rowland. Nell briefly wondered what had been done with Rowland, if he was not wearing his leash, but became aware of a silence as Eleanor was busy staring at the amazing donkey with her mouth open.

Mrs. Troyd sunk her head in her hands briefly; the movement caught Eleanor's eye and she hurriedly finished. "Er they travelled long and far, and when they got to Bethlehem, Mary was tired, but so many people had already got there that it was very difficult to find a room for the night." She gathered her papers and climbed down from the lectern, while Rachel Clark and Patty Brett took their places at the other side of the stage.

Steven and Jenny dragged the donkey across the stage to the Innkeeper, played by Rachel, with Patty as Innkeeper's Wife.

"What a long journey that was! I am very tired from walking all that way and I am worried about poor Mary who is near her time! If we do not get a room in the inn, it will be very difficult. Here is an inn, I wonder if they have any rooms left. Knock knock!" Steven knocked on the wooden chair, and then remembered himself. "Er, I mean—" He knocked again, with an apologetic look at Mrs. Troyd.

Rachel stepped forward. "What do you want?"

"I want a room for the night. My wife is heavy with child and we have nowhere to stay."

"Well you can't stay here—there's no room at the inn!" Rachel thundered. Mrs. Troyd frowned at her and Rachel sent her an apologetic look, remembering that she was not supposed to be employing quite this much gusto. Steven and Jenny made a great show of looking sad and walked off to do a circuit of the altar, with much clacking of Steven's shoes.

"Ooooh, Joseph, I hope we can find a room soon." Jenny clutched at her cushion with her spare hand theatrically as she dragged the donkey (now on its side) behind them. "For I am up the duff and my baby is coming soon."

Steven clattered over to the microphone again, and the quicker-witted wearers of hearing-aids clapped their hands over their ears. "PERHAPS THERE WILL BE A ROOM AT THIS INN!" He clacked over to Rachel again. "Knoc—Ha!" He caught himself and grinned triumphantly at Nell, before knocking with a flourish on the wooden chair.

"What is it?" Rachel stood forward again, Patty beside her this time.

"My wife is up the duff an' the baby is comin' soon an' can we have a room please?" Steven improvised, having forgotten his words slightly in his triumph.

"There is no room at the inn..." Rachel purred, saccharine, which was somehow far more gloating than before.

"Oh dear, my time is close at hand. Is there nowhere we can stay?" Jenny was having to hold the cushion in place now as it had started on a slow but inexorable downwards slide.

Patty stepped forward, looked at the sea of faces in front of her, and was consumed with nerves. "Mmm mmm mmm" was all that could be heard. She glanced at Nell, who was miming that she should shout, and tried again, but "Jebediah mmm mmm mmm" was as much as she could manage. Nell gave her commiseratory smile and nodded at Rachel to continue.

"Well, I suppose there's always the stable," Rachel shrugged. "You could stay there—it's warm and safe and you'd have it all to yourself apart from the animals."

Steven clacked back over to the microphone. "YES PLEASE!"

So while Nell, Maria Effle, and Melanie Brett moved the props onto the stage, Rachel and Patty led a circuit round the altar, with Steven clattering after them and Jenny at the end, clutching her cushion with one hand and dragging a scarlet tinsel-festooned donkey on a lead with the other.

By the time they had got round, the Stable had been constructed—an area of raised staging to the side of the altar, it was separated from the main action by a "wall" made of sheets of brick-patterned wallpaper plastered over a clothes horse. There was a small wooden box of hay in the middle with a chair to either side. Steven and Jenny took their place in these, though there was just a suspicion of congregational sniggering when Jenny let go of the cushion. It dropped out of her dress and, no fool she, she pounced on it and, putting it on the hard wooden chair, made a show of getting comfortable on it, to Steven's silent disgust.

Rachel now mounted the lectern to do her own stint as Narrator, as Eleanor was imminently due onstage. "Mary and Joseph were very grateful to have found somewhere safe to stay, as Mary's time was very near; so the innkeeper led them into the stable where they could be comfy and warm."

There was a brief pause before an expert elbow was applied to the ribs of Albert Oddleton, the parish organist, by his wife, and then he accompanied as the children sang "Away in a Manger."

Emma and Abigail, sweet little angels that they were, exited the back room with a plastic Baby Jesus. Emma snatched it from

Abigail, who grabbed it back, but at a glare from Mrs. Troyd, she ungraciously extended an extremity to Emma who took it equally ungraciously, and they marched crossly down one aisle and up the other, getting to the stable when the second verse was still only starting. They climbed up the staging and held the Baby Jesus forward to Jenny, only then realising they were holding the doll's legs, not its arms.

"See? I tole you she always carries it wrong!" Emma scolded. They sat cross-legged on the staging in front of the manger, and Abigail pointedly turned her back on Emma and sat facing the side.

As the singing continued, Mrs. Troyd was frantically trying to catch Rachel's eye and indicate that as there were currently no shepherds, she should jump a bit; however, being slightly nervous, she was reading through the next bit rather than paying attention to the singing, so the second verse finished without Rachel having received this message.

"And so the Baby Jesus was born in a stable and was laid in a crib for a bed. Up on a nearby hillside, Shepherds were watching their sheep when all of a sudden there was a bright light in the darkness."

Michael leapt onto the stage and looked at Rachel and then at Mrs Troyd. He shrugged and improvised.

"I am the Angel Gabriel an' I come to tell some shepherds about the Baby Jesus—"

There was a slam and the church door was thrown open. A tufty-headed, spangle-jeaned figure sprinted up the aisle and skidded to a stop on the stage, looking most out of place in the context of the other children's costumes.

"A—a shepherd's life is quiet an' dull," Lizzie Willikins panted, "an' I have been sitting on this hillside watching my sheep all day an' nothing much has happened. But suddenly I woke up an' there was this light shining on the hillside." She paused to catch another breath, holding her side where she'd developed a stitch. "I wonder what it can be?"

"I am the Angel Gabriel," Michael repeated, "an' like I was sayin', I come to tell you that a child has been born to us, the son of God come to save us and he is Christ the King!"

"Where is this baby?" Lizzie was starting to breathe a little more normally now. "Tell me that I may come and worship. I shall bring him my pet lamb for a present—" She turned round to where Stephanie should have been and was dismayed to find an empty stage.

"She in't here, she's off poorly," hissed Michael. Daisy, seeing a salvation, chucked her cuddly Shaun the Sheep onto the stage. Lizzie turned to glance despairingly at Mrs. Troyd, and that lady having her head in her hands again, Nell shrugged and gestured at her to pick it up.

"I shall bring him my... Shaun the Sheep for a present," Lizzie continued dubiously. She and Michael regarded its pop-eyed stare for a moment, while in the back of the church, Mike Hill was sniggering into his moustache again.

"Prob'ly better," Michael shrugged. "Can't do much with a real sheep anyhow." And the two of them walked off with Shaun the Sheep.

WE THREE KINGS OF ORIENT ARE

*R*achel, at the lectern, was watching Melanie Brett helping Lucy frantically try to fit the crown over her topknot and tie on the cloak at the same time. The silence recalled her to her job, however, and she picked up her script, found her place, and hastily went on.

"In the East at this time, there were three wise men. They watched the stars and could foretell many great things that were to happen. One day the First King went to see the Second King."

Eleanor was in place at one side of the stage, and Lucy dashed off to the other, cloak askew and crown only staying on because it was held in place by the ponytail on the top of her skull which fountained through the middle of the crown and bobbed over her right ear jauntily. She leapt onto the stage, spangly trousers a-twinkle, and adopted a position of deep meditation, shading her eyes and gazing up at an imaginary sky.

"Melchisedech," she greeted Eleanor gravely.

"Balthasar, it is long since we last met."

"Is it the star that has brought you?"

"Yes—such a star must have great significance. What do you think it means?"

"Let us confer with… with …" Lucy forgot the name of the Third king, scrabbled, and came up with another king-type Arabian name from a recent visit to the theatre. "With Abanazar."

"With Abanazar?" Eleanor gaped.

"Did someone call for me? For I am Abanazar, the King of Skiing!" Suzanna stepped onto the stage with a flourish, flittering mascara'd eyelashes in her panda-tan. Mike Hill guffawed out loud before he could stop himself, and his wife slapped his arm, though her shoulders were shaking suspiciously too.

Mrs. Troyd simply stared. It had not occurred to her that the lovely Suzanna would not have learned the lines for the Third King (as there were only two of them to learn) but never in her wildest dreams would she have suggested that Suzanna would simply take them off-script in this way.

"What?" Lucy looked for help but found none; Mrs. Troyd was gobsmacked, and Nell appeared to be silently weeping into her script. Poor Nell! Lucy thought, and realised that it was up to her to save the day. Besides she was wearing spangly jeans.

"Yes, Abanazar, we wanted to ask you about the star…" Lucy elbowed Eleanor, galvanising her into action.

"Er, yeah, Abanazar, that bright one… er…"

"It is a star of great significance," Suzanna said solemnly. "And we should follow where it leads, because that would be the wise thing to do and we are the Three Queens."

"We are not Queens, we're Kings!" hissed Lucy.

"How can we be Kings? We're girls." Suzanna put one hand on her hip. "Anyhow we've got shiny cloaks and crowns and everything, so we must be Queens because Kings with all dresses on would look like girls anyhow. And Kings would have beards and horses and swords. Have you got a beard and a horse and a sword, because I haven't. But I have got a crown and a shiny cloak and a pretty dress with ribbons on, so I must be a Queen. And I'm the Queen of Skiing because I just went skiing and I was really good at it and I went on the grown-up slopes and the instructor said I was really brave and everything and, besides, I've got a skier's tan and you haven't, so I must be the Queen of Skiing."

This being something of a conversational brick, Lucy fell silent in the sort of amazement normally employed by shepherds confronted by an angel. However, by this time, Eleanor had rallied somewhat.

"Very well, Abanazar, you can be the Queen of Skiing but Lucy and I are Wise Men and we're going to follow that star to see where the Baby Jesus lies."

"I might come with you," Suzanna shrugged. "There isn't much else to do here. They haven't invented the telly or Playstations or Wii or anything yet. Anyway, babies are soooooo cuuuute!!"

And with another fluttering of her panda-eyes, she followed the others round the altar where they picked up their presents and went on to the Stable. Maisie Oddleton's elbow making contact with Albert's ribs, the organist jerked into life with the strains of "We Three Kings," and as the three girls wandered round the altar, Eleanor gave a large gold box to Mary and bowed.

Emma, sitting on the front of the stage, poked Abigail in the ribs. "That's that spoon. It's in a posh box an' all!"

Her stage whisper was amplified over the children's singing by the microphone nearby.

Lucy gave over a blue box, and bowed, and Abigail, who had by now completely forgotten that she was not speaking to her friend, turned to ask, "Is that the teddy bear?"

"Noooooo, silly, it's not a teddy bear, it's a Frankenstein— y'know, like a man but green with a thing in his neck."

"And that's the rusks then?"

Even Suzanna stopped to send her a puzzled glance at that, handing over the shiny green box with an elaborate curtsey as she had learned to do it at ballet. The three of them squashed carefully between Steven's chair and the rickety clothes-horse wall and arrayed themselves in the background. Suzanna made a great show of sitting down on the edge and arranging the satin of her skirt and the shiny cloak to best advantage, and then assumed an expression of great piety as was appropriate to the dignity of Abanazar, Queen of Skiing.

Eleanor being tallest, stood at the back, and Lucy sidled in between them. She was very red in the face and was not feeling at all well. Having taken full advantage of the party buffet, she had eaten three packs of Sour Squigglers, a Sherbet Exploder, most of a Popping Candy Party Pack, and a Whistling Dayglo-Pop, as well as four servings of green jelly and ice cream. On top of all that she had snaffled copious glasses of Tizer while her mother was not there to forbid that particular delight, and now she was beginning to wish that she had not run from the car with quite so fast.

"O-oh star of wonder star of night," the children sang. Lucy belched quietly and Steven started to snigger.

"Star with royal beauty bright."

She started to feel very odd indeed.

"Westward leading, still proceeding—"

Nell saw her expression and jumped up, dashing out of the pew just in time to grab the Baby Jesus out of the crib as Lucy threw up in it. Throwing the doll at Jenny, Nell was joined by Melanie Brett, who glanced at the manger and suggested, "Later."

"Yes," Nell agreed, and while Melanie helped poor Lucy off the stage, her ponytail still bobbing perkily over her ear rather at odds with the rest of her demeanour, Nell whispered to Steven to pass over his tea towel (he took off the head-dress with great alacrity) which she draped over the crib to hide the contents, and then as the music was finishing, told the children quietly, "We're nearly finished now; let's not spoil it. Just go on as normal—but don't put the baby in the manger!!" Nell sat down again and as the music stopped, the children all glanced at each other.

"That's disgustin', that is, she barfed in the crib!" Emma muttered, right into the microphone. "Dun't 'alf stink. Makin' me gip, that is." But catching Mrs. Troyd's eye, she subsided again.

"Thank you for these lovely gifts!" Jenny's sudden improvisation made them all jump but did bring them back on-course. "The red one and the green one and the blue one. I can't open them now because I have to hold the Baby Jesus, what with the manger being all full of upchuck an' everythin', but it was very kind."

Suzanna jumped up and curtsied again. "You're welcome!" She flashed a big fake smile at the audience. "Him being the Son of God, it seemed wise to get on his good side, and we are the Three Wise Men after all! Well, they are, anyway. I'm not a King, I am Abanazar the Wise Queen of Skiing, you can tell by my skier's tan."

They considered this.

"Dun't sound very wise to me to end up lookin' like a panda," Emma muttered, and again it was broadcast across the church. There was a high-pitched squeak from the corner where the Hill family sat with covered faces and shaking shoulders, all having lost it by now. Michael shook his head, disgusted, and whispered "In't there a bit with the Stable Song now?"

"Oooh!" Rachel stopped watching and grabbed her script. "Yeah, there is too! Er, Jesus was surrounded by the animals who were happy to let him sleep in their manger—er, who would have been happy to let him sleep in their manger if the shepherd han't been sick in it—and the Kings and Abanazar and the shepherds looked on in wonder. Except the shepherd's in the back room chucking up, so she isn't looking on in wonder. At least not at the baby…." Rachel's voice faltered to a stop as Mrs. Troyd stared daggers at her, and in the background, there was a great shuffling of paper as once again the organist was nudged out of his snooze and galvanised into action by means of his wife's elbow, and then he began to play the music for the Stable Song.

DING DONG MERRILY ON HIGH

*D*aisy shuffled onto the stage, fetching in her cow hat and black-blotched T-shirt. She was holding a Shaun the Sheep and grabbed at the scarlet donkey to ensure that all the relevant animals were present and correct, but it appeared to be snagged on something and she gave it a mighty tug. Jenny nearly fell off her chair; she was still holding the donkey's lead, and let go of it in a hurry, sending an evil look at poor Daisy, who whispered "Sorry!" loudly and grabbed the donkey to her; however its head had been wrenched and lolled at an unnatural angle, still with sombrero and jolly tinsel hatband. The audience tittered and Mrs. Troyd covered her eyes briefly as the children began to sing.

"In a stable in Bethlehem long ago
 A baby was born 'mid the ice and snow
 For Mary and Joseph had no place to go
 But the stable was nice and warm."

It was probably unlikely that there had been much of a blizzard in Palestine, Nell thought as she recovered her composure, but that was hardly the point. Daisy was visibly psyching herself up for this solo, unexpected and a bit unsettling given that she had expected to be accompanied by Stephanie as the sheep and Joseph Willikins as the donkey, rather than a Shaun the Sheep toy and a Spanish hat-wearing donkey.

THE CHILDREN WENT ON SINGING:
"The animals stood in the straw and hay;
They knew that this was a special day,
and looked at the manger where the baby lay
For the Saviour Christ was born."

IT WAS time for the chorus and Daisy was working up to her "moo".

"SO THE COW SAID—"
"MOO" she shrieked at a pitch to shatter glass.
"—and the sheep said BAA—" (She waved the Shaun the sheep.)
"And the donkey stamped his hoof!" (The children all stamped and Steven looked very pleased at the clackety effect of his football boots while Daisy dropped the Shaun and picked the sombrero'd donkey up and waved that).
"And Joseph said—"
The music fell to a stop while Steven clacked over to the microphone and boomed "HUSHHHHH!"
"As the doves cooed in the roof."

"THE SHEPHERDS into the stable went

The Three Wise Kings by the star were sent
The angels there by the manger leant
But the stable was nice and warm."

(WHICH WAS a bit of a non sequitur, but Nell had never found lack of coherency to be a huge sticking point in children's plays; it was outweighed by the cuteness factor every time.)

"MARY SAT in the stable stall;
　　Joseph stood by the old stone wall;
　　Wonder and reverence filled them all
　　For the Saviour Christ was born."

DAISY SUDDENLY CLAPPED a hand to her mouth. For a split second Nell thought she was going to be sick, but the girl had suddenly remembered something, and had the look of someone who has thought of a solution, is not at all sure that it is the correct one, but hasn't got time to come up with a plan B. Nell was filled with foreboding.

"THE COW SAID—"

"ROWLAND!" Daisy shrieked, most unexpectedly. "You're supposed to be the dog-sheep! Here Rowland!"

"And the sheep said—"

"Arff! Arfff afff affff!" Rowland barked, bounding delighted out of the back room where he had been curled up asleep and dashing up onto the stage where Daisy was. The singing dissolved into chaos as the great shaggy hound leapt and wagged and dashed about.

"And the don... key..." Some of the children tried to keep

singing but there was not much room in the Stable, and as Rowland dashed and leapt, he pushed Eleanor backwards.

"...stamped his hoof..."

Eleanor slipped off the edge of the staging, pulling the clothes-horse wall with her and dragging Suzanna, who stared in horror as her shiny satin dress ripped on the corner of the staging.

"And Jo... seph said—"

(The hearing aid wearers clapped their hands over their ears.)

Clack clack clack clack. "HUSSSSSHHHHH!"

"Arfff arrfff arfff grrrrrroowwwwwwllllll!"

"No! That's me dad's best donkey! Gerrrittoffim!"

"As the doves cooed on the roof."

The music faded and Jenny dived across the staging to grab the donkey from the dog. "Give it 'ere, you mangy beast!" Jenny put her entire weight into the tug, then went staggering back across the staging. Michael caught her just before she fell off the edge and she held it up triumphantly. "I got 'im!!!"

"Noooo... you pulled 'is 'ead off! Me dad's best donkey!" Michael howled, snatching the decapitated beast from her and casting a poisonous look at the infamous Rowland, who was chewing away at the sombrero'd head with a look of intense grati-fication and spitting out bits of tinsel.

"No need to grab it, I was just helpin'!" Jenny snapped back.

Daisy was looking deeply offended. "My dog Rowland is a good dog an' he is not a mangy beast an' Mrs. Troyd said he could be a dog-sheep!"

Nell stood up at this point, and the children all fell quiet. Melanie Brett called Rowland to her, Eleanor helped Suzanna out of the wreckage of the stable wall where she was quietly snivelling at the damage to her dress, and at a nod from Nell and the judi-cious application of his wife's elbow, Albert started to play and the children all scrambled back into place, to sing "Silent Night".

After a few moments' commotion, the congregation joined in just in time for the second line.

"All is calm, all is quiet…" For some reason the first verse was very ragged and seemed to involve more than the usual amount of coughing, not to mention a surprisingly large number of people wiping away tears; however, by the second verse everyone had calmed down a bit more, and by the end of Silent Night, when Albert segued into "Ding Dong Merrily on High" the singing was nearer its usual standards.

Soon it all drew to a close, and Father Hume mounted the lectern. For a moment he simply gazed at the congregation with a wry look on his face before shaking his head ruefully. "What can I say about this year's play?"

The congregation went into hysterics, and though he did keep a straight face, Nell noticed a distinct twitch to the corners of his mouth.

"What an act to follow! Mrs. Troyd, Nell, it has been a joy to watch. Children, you have done very well to keep things going, and I have been delighted to see your understanding of the Christmas story. I have to say,"—and here he dropped all attempt to go into the usual speech, leant on the lectern and gazed at the congregation over his half-moon glasses—"I don't think I've enjoyed a Christmas play so much in years. Let's have a round of applause for everyone involved!"

The church erupted in hearty applause and a certain amount of giggling. Daisy, Emma, and Abigail got up and disappeared into the back room at a gesture from the Priest, reappearing with wrapped presents which they gave to Mrs. Troyd, Nell, and Maria Effle.

("Do you think these ones are gold, Frankenstein, and myrrh too?"

"Nooooo, silly, these ones are sherry—y'know, what's in that goblet thing at communion. It's good stuff, my dad says.")

Father Hume went on, "Wine and mince pies will be served in the Parish rooms now, so I hope we'll see you all over there."

He climbed down from the lectern and there was a last round of applause, though a bit more uncertainly this time because one never knows whether clapping in church is quite allowed unless prompted by the priest, and then it all dissolved into chattering and laughing as the parishioners filed out into the aisle and the children inveigled their way through the crowd to find their own parents.

HERE WE COME A-WASSAILING

There was a moment of silence in the front pew as Nell and Maria collapsed back in their seats with relief.

"Well, they seemed to enjoy that," Nell said brightly.

"I certainly did, aye." Maria grinned.

"Nell, Maria, I'd like to thank you for your help." Mrs. Troyd told them, standing up. "Please accept these." She handed them a little present, each beautifully wrapped with a pretty gold bow on them.

"Thank you, Mrs. T!"

"Thank you very much!"

"Are you coming in for a glass of wine?" Mrs. Troyd paused in the gathering of bag and coat.

"Yes, I think so."

"Then I shall see you in there."

Nell watched Mrs. Troyd leave, graciously accepting congratulations all the way down the aisle, and then she caught Maria's eye.

"Shall we?" Maria nudged her in the ribs.

"Open them?"

"Yes, see what they are?"

Nell looked at her friend for a moment; the mischief in Maria's eyes was infectious, and she began to laugh.

"Oh go on then!"

The two of them pulled open the bows and the wrapping paper unfurled to reveal Nell's present, a rather pretty china cup, and Maria's present, a small box containing a little green bird-shaped ornament.

"How lovely!" Nell picked the cup up, admiring the pattern of flowers and berries on it.

"Eh, in't that nice?" Maria opened the clear plastic bit of the box to take the little ornament out. The bird was firmly lodged in place, and when she tugged at it, it brought out the shaped polystyrene in which it was embedded. Maria put the box down and pulled the ornament out of its packaging, but when she did so, a small shiny piece of card fluttered to the floor.

Nell set her cup down on the pew and picked it up. As she did so, she caught sight of writing on the other side, and paused to read what it said.

"To My Favourite Teacher, from Emelda XXXXX"

Maria read it over her shoulder. "Well, it just goes to show, dun't it?"

Nell looked at her friend, hoping she wasn't too upset, but Maria was grinning broadly.

"Does it?" Nell asked.

"Aye—I never knew she were that into recyclin'!" And the two of them went into helpless laughter.

"I SEE she left you two with all the clearing up again. Want a hand wi' that?"

Wiping her eyes, Nell turned to find Mike Hill behind them. "Oh thank you, Mike, that would be very kind." Nell and Mike began to clear up the debris of the stable while Maria collected together various bits of costume and props. "I daren't ask if you enjoyed that," Nell ventured with a mischievous grin, which he returned, twinkling at her.

"I 'aven't laughed so much in years!"

"Your Michael was very good, you know," she went on. "He knew every line off by heart almost from the first practice when he took over as the angel. He might have elaborated a bit in the actual performance, but he put a lot of work into it."

"Aye, 'e does that when 'e gets a notion into 'is 'ead." Mike was quietly proud as a peacock.

"Oh dear, Mike!" Melanie Brett came dashing over with Rowland, now safely back on his lead. "I am so sorry about your donkey! Michael says you're very attached to it. Perhaps we can replace it somehow? I mean, I know you can never replace the sentimental value, but at least we could replace the donkey?"

Mike glanced round and saw Michael watching anxiously from the other side of the church.

"You goin' across for a glass of wine, right? Can we talk about it over there, Mel? I'm just helping wi' t' clearing up."

"Yes, certainly, sorry Mike." Melanie flustered away, with Rowland still trying to get the enticingly chewable donkey-head from her hand.

"Aw, no, 'e's really upset," Michael muttered to Alex le Grand, with whom he was chatting. "Me Nan give 'im that donkey, all the way from Torramaleeenoes."

"I bet you could get a new one though." Alex looked thoughtful. "You can get everything on the internet these days."

Michael brightened at this thought. "Yeah... I could do some jobs, wash the car and that. They give me money for that sometimes, and 'is birthday is in March, so I reckon I could save up and get 'im a new one for then. Good idea, Alex!" He elbowed his friend appreciatively. "'Ey, you gonna come in for a mince pie?"

"Too right!" Alex grinned, and gathering his crutches and his Power Monkey paraphernalia, he hobbled out in search of seasonal pastries.

ARIANNA LE GRAND watched him go, a troubled look on her face. "Do you think we ought to let him spend time with that boy?"

Harry le Grand shot her an old-fashioned look. "Of course we should; Alex is shy and doesn't have many friends. Michael seems like a kind lad. I don't know why you'd even ask."

"Well...." Arianna coughed delicately. "I wouldn't like him to pick up such provincial speech patterns, Harry."

"Don't be such a snob, my girl!" Harry was exasperated. "And anyhow, when we took him to Germany, did he pick up German? He did not, despite several days of highly expensive lessons."

"That is true..."

"Face it, Arianna, he has a tin ear for language."

"Perhaps it will develop later," she mused, and strode off after her son.

"Perhaps it won't," Harry growled. Mike Hill passing by at that moment, Harry called after him. "'Scuse me, you're Michael's dad, aren't you?"

"I am that; and Alex is your lad, is he?"

"He is indeed." Harry hesitated, then threw caution to the winds. Arianna might not approve but Alex assuredly would, and it was time that boy got a break. Well, one not of a bone-related type, anyway. "Listen, your Michael likes these damn monkey cartoons that Alex is so fond of. Arianna wouldn't let him stop at home and watch the Christmas special, so I set it to record. If your lad would like to come over and watch it, I think Alex would enjoy the company."

Mike twinkled. "I'll ask 'im, but I think 'e'll be made up."

"Excellent." Harry grinned, correctly surmising that this was a good thing. "Apart from anything else, it'll be a good excuse for me to send the women across to the mother-in-law's without having to go with them."

Mike nodded appreciatively. "A man with a plan, I see! You comin' across the way?"

"Yes; Arianna's already across there so I suspect I'm driving, but the mince pies are always good."

NELL WATCHED the two from across the church as they headed off; two equally quiet pleasant men, the one resigned to the vagaries of his wife and the other running his family with a light rein. She suspected they'd get on as well as their boys seemed to. She did a last whisk round the church, checking for props and other misplaced articles before she left the deacon to lock up, and then wandered across to the parish rooms for the usual post-play mince pie.

The parish rooms were packed, the air thick with the rich, heavy scent of alcohol and cinnamon. Nell's taste ran more to sweet sherry than the dry, slightly acidic white wine they tended to serve on these occasions, so she took a glass of orange juice and stood to one side, watching the scene before her.

In the centre of the room, Mrs. Troyd, of course, her bouquet splendid in the centre of the table; various of the stalwarts of the parish were clustered round her, giving their congratulations on the play.

To the other side of centre, Arianna le Grand, artfully placed on the little raised platform, waited for Harry to bring her a refill while Suzanna prattled and declared, all blonde ringlets, fluttering eyelashes, and panda-tan. Arianna was only half-listening, agreeing absently with her daughter as she regally surveyed the room and nodded graciously as Nell caught her eye.

Harry le Grand had not reached the queue for refills yet, however, as he had stopped to have a word with Alex and Michael. Nell could not hear what it was he was saying but the boys were evidently delighted by it.

In another corner, the older girls were fussing over Rowland, who, far from being in disgrace, had proved the star of the show. Steven was kicking around a polystyrene cup till he tripped and stood on it, spiking it on his football boots. He stood on one leg to retrieve it, but every time he bent forward, he lost his balance, and eventually sat down on the floor in great disgust and pulled it free.

In front of them, the long-suffering Mr. Willikins was packing up Lizzie and Lucy Melcombe to drop them off home. Lucy had spilt juice on her spangly jeans and Lizzie's ponytail was less vertical than it had been; both were hyper from an excess of Sour Squigglers but were still cheerful with it. Mr. Melcombe had only just rung through to say the AA had turned up and were dropping the car off at the nearest garage.

Further down the room, much laughter from the table where Maria Effle and the Hill family sat. Nell watched for a moment but could not resist wandering over, snaffling another mince pie as she passed.

"Nell! Do come and join us!" Maria shifted the bouquet she had received from the chair and Nell sat down.

"You timed that well, Nell, I'm just doing a drinks run!" Mary Hill smiled. "Does anyone want a refill while I'm going past?"

"I'm fine thank you." Nell looked down to see the iniquitous Rowland had wandered over. Mike patted his leg and the dog flopped down in front of him, regarding him with soulful eyes.

"Who's a good old doggie then?" Mike ruffled the hound's head and it leant against him adoringly. "Who's a good old boy?"

"You're very forgiving, Mike," Nell observed, watching him feed the dog a bit of mince pie. "Considering he just dismembered your donkey, I mean."

Mike looked round, checking that Mary was out of earshot.

"Aye, and a great relief that was, an' all! It were a present from the mother-in-law so I din't like to let on, but I never liked that damn thing. What does a grown man want with a big red donkey, I ask you? An' with that bloody awful 'at an' all. When I saw young

Rowland 'ere chomping on its 'ead, I wanted to applaud. Every cloud, eh?" He winked at Nell, who laughed out loud while Maria slapped him on the back.

"You're a wily one, Mike! Whose suggestion was it to use the donkey in the play?"

Mike looked very innocent. "It was in the interests of Mrs. Troyd's best Nativity," he announced loftily. "A public service, it was."

Melanie Brett came over at that point with the children.

"Mike, about the donkey."

"Don't you worry, love," Mike grinned. "Me and Rowland 'ave 'ad a talk and 'e says 'e won't do any such thing again." He ruffled the dog's head and it rolled onto its back to have its tummy tickled. "See? We're the best of friends, 'im and me."

"Listen, I have to go now and get the turkey on." Melanie gestured at Patty who went to put the lead on Rowland. "But we should talk about this another time."

"Tell you what, Mel, I'll catch you in the Rose an' Crown sometime and you can buy me a pint. Then we'll be quits. Deal?"

"Deal..." Melanie was not convinced but gave the lead to Patty and made her goodbyes. "Patty, make sure that someone has hold of that lead all the time, will you? If you want to go and play, then ask Rachel or Mrs. Clark to keep a hold of him, just like always." On the way out, she came across Michael, and with a quick glance back into the room to see that his father was not watching, she stopped briefly.

"Michael, how attached was your Dad to that donkey? I feel really bad about it and he said it was fine but I don't know if he was just being nice, so I was hoping you might be able to tell me. Does he really like it or do you think he genuinely doesn't mind?"

Michael looked solemn. "It was 'is best donkey, what me Nan brought him all the way from Torramaleenoes, Mrs. Brett. 'E's always been dead careful with it. 'E keeps it in the spare room so it dun't get knocked over or owt. But it's 'is birthday in March, and I was thinkin' they might 'ave one on the internet somewhere."

"Oh! Oh right, what a good idea! Thank you very much for that, Michael, it was really kind of you to tell me." Melanie was really dismayed to think that she had destroyed a beloved souvenir and determined to find a replacement. Mike was such a nice man and had taken it so well; if it took her till March, she would find him one just like it! And vowing to see it done, she marched off to see to the turkey.

GOD REST YE MERRY GENTLEMEN...

*B*ack in the room and unaware of the interesting manner in which his birthday was shaping up, Mike looked down at Patty. "You not goin' with your mum?"

"We're stoppin' on a bit," Patty whispered. "We're goin' home with Jenny an' Emma."

"Is it secret? Shhh! Don't tell anyone!" Mike teased, whispering back.

Patty dimpled up at him. "NO, MISTER HILL, IT IN'T A SECRET!"

Conversation stopped for a moment as everyone looked round. Patty blushed mightily as Nell and Maria applauded. "Next year, Patty, if you can say all your lines like that, we might find a few more for you to say perhaps. Would you like that?"

Patty considered. "Can I be like an angel, Miss, but a funny one?"

"A funny one?" Nell exchanged glances with Maria.

"Yes, Miss, a funny one."

"Well, we'd have to ask Mrs. Troyd about that, but if there is a play with a funny angel in it, Patty, I can just see you playing that part."

Satisfied, Patty nodded, dimpled, and went back to tell the other girls, Rowland following, wagging amicably.

"A funny angel?" Maria shook her head. "What would that entail?"

"The mind boggles...!"

"Ah well; that's enough excitement for me for one day," Maria got to her feet. "People are starting to leave; there'll be glasses to wash."

One by one, people filed out of the parish rooms, stopping by Father Hume to wish him a Happy Christmas as they went. Nell and Mike went to free the deacon from the toils of the hoover, which as usual had sprung unhooked at an unexpected moment and floored him as he attempted to hoover in the church, and brought him into the warmth of the parish rooms.

The children congregated on the stairs outside the building, swinging on the handrail like festive little monkeys, hyper to varying degrees on a mince pie-induced sugar rush, and apparently oblivious to the cold in the way that only children are.

Mrs. Troyd said her goodbyes and left. She went to the car in which her long-suffering husband was waiting, listening to Radio 4 patiently. She put her bags in the back and extracted a single yellow rose from the bouquet. Mr. Troyd turned the engine off and got out. He came round the car, locking it as they walked back to the darkened churchyard, and Mrs. Troyd slipped her arm through his in the chilly night, and kissed him on the cheek. They opened the wicket gate and disappeared into the winter evening.

Nell turned away from the window. This little ceremony happened every year. Few people were aware of it but one year she had cut through the graveyard on the way home, and had seen the couple lay their flower on the grave. As she watched, they said some words, patted the little gravestone briefly and left to go home. When they were out of sight, she had gone to look and in the fading light, had read the legend:

"Evelyn Troyd: 1966-1971. Our little angel."

Feeling she had intruded on something private, she had never mentioned it, but every Christmas, she watched the Troyds go to tell their daughter how the play had been and wish her a Merry Christmas.

Now, the engine of the car outside told her that they had returned, and were on their way back to the warmth of their quiet little bungalow, and the parish rooms were getting quite empty. Nell too made her goodbyes and walked out with Mrs. Clark, who was in search of the children.

"Goodnight Nell! Happy Christmas!" Mrs. Clark called after her, then shivered in the rapidly chilling evening. "Emma, Abigail, we'll be going in about ten minutes. Goodness, aren't you cold?"

"Nah, we got our coats on, Mum." Emma shrugged. "'Snot that cold anyhow."

"Okay then. Is there anything you've left inside?"

"Mrs. Effle took the angel dresses, Mrs. Clark, but she said we could keep the haloes 'cos we looked just like little angels in 'em," Abigail replied.

"Quite right too. Well, if you two are ready to go, you can stay out here while I get the others sorted if you want? Then we'll all walk up together with Rowland."

"Cool," Emma watched Nell go on her way, then turned back to gaze moodily across the car park until another thought struck her. "Where is a Chelsea stable anyhow?"

Abigail was puzzled. "Dunno. Why?"

"Well, it's in the song in't it? About the girl in the stable?"

"What, Mary?"

"Nooooo, not her, the other one."

"What other one?"

"Gloria. Y'know, Gloria in a Chelsea Stable. I just wondered where a Chelsea Stable was."

"Dunno. Next to the Bethlehem Stable, I s'pose." With which pronouncement Abigail shrugged, and the two of them bit into the last of their mince pies.

ABOUT THE AUTHOR

Dulcie Feenan lives in a small village in the North of England. She has been involved in her local parish for many years in various guises, and has had much enjoyment from being a part of the community. However, she declines to write under her normal name for fear of ending up on the Women's Institute Most Wanted List. (They already know that she puts the wrong kind of jam on her Victoria Sponges… another infraction might be a step too far.)

www.ingramcontent.com/pod-product-compliance
Lightning Source LLC
Chambersburg PA
CBHW020551130626
46552CB00007B/2863